Levi

THE STANTON PACK BOOK 5

KATHI S. BARTON

This is a work of fiction. Names, characters, places, and incidents are products of the author's imagination or are used fictitiously and are not to be construed as real. Any resemblance to actual events, locations, organizations, or persons, living or dead, is entirely coincidental.

World Castle Publishing, LLC
Pensacola, Florida
Copyright © Kathi S. Barton 2019
Paperback ISBN: 9781949812855
eBook ISBN: 9781949812862
First Edition World Castle Publishing, LLC, April 8, 2019
http://www.worldcastlepublishing.com
Licensing Notes
Cover: Karen Fuller
Editor: Maxine Bringenberg

Chapter 1

Hailey held Ray's hand and thought about what Denny had told her today. He'd been taking over her care since they'd gotten back to the house, and it had worked out well for her and Ray. Taking her to the doctor every couple of days would have been hard on her.

"He destroyed her womb. There isn't any chance that she'll be able to carry a child and keep it. There has been much too much damage done for her to even take the chance. When she's better, and I have to believe that she will get there, she should think about having a sterilization surgery done to prevent it from happening." She asked Denny if it would hurt her to get pregnant. "Yes, it could very well kill her."

Now here she sat with her friend, wondering what she was going to do with that information. Reaching out to Levi, who was still in France, she smiled when he laughed before speaking. They had become very close over the last week, and she was glad that he was happy.

I took your advice, and I can't thank you enough for it. I went and found some of the smaller, off the chart galleries, and had a blast. There are so many different things out there to see and create that I found myself buying things just because they were so unique. She laughed at his enthusiasm. *Don't be surprised if a large crate comes your way soon. I thought about waiting and bringing it home with me, but I couldn't wait for you to see my finds. How is your friend?*

No change. But your dad told me that she wasn't going to be able to hold a child of her own. It breaks my heart how people treat their children. What would possess a man to do this to his own child? Not to mention what my mother did to hers. She felt her heart crumble for the pain of her stepfamily's deaths. *Cheer me up, Levi. Tell me some adventure that you've had since I spoke to you last.*

I'm so sorry, Hailey. She knew that he'd understand if she couldn't answer him. *Yesterday I had an encounter with one of the artists. I tell you, Hailey, I'm glad in that moment that you or the rest of the women weren't with me. You would surely have cut him down. He was so pissed that I wasn't buying anything from his booth when I was shopping.*

What did he sell? He was laughing hard, and it made her laugh too. *Oh, I have a feeling this is going to be really good.*

I swear to you, it looked like he went and got him some wood out of the small parks around here and hot glued — I kid you not — he hot glued shells all over the pieces so that not one bit of the wood was showing. There were places on it that he might have run out of shells, so he drew them on some paper and stuck them there. I swear to you, it was only beautiful to those like him. I don't think he sold a single stick. She asked if he was making that up. And as soon as he started laughing again, her phone made a noise telling her that she had a message. *See it? I had to sneak that picture. He has several signs in his booth that say no pictures. Why, I have no idea, but there you have it.*

She laughed even harder after seeing the picture, and she was so glad that Levi had told her about it. After they talked for a bit longer, really him only telling her what he'd been enjoying, Levi told her that he had an appointment and needed to get going.

When are you coming home? He said that he was leaving in two days. *I can't wait to see you, Levi. I have a big hug here waiting for you.*

Hailey squeezed Ray's hand, and was shocked when it felt like she had given her a returning squeeze. Trying it again, she also floated into her head to see if she was awake yet, and saw that her mind was going over the day at her office.

Ray? She stilled for a moment in her memories. *Ray, it's Hailey. Do you remember me? I'd like to talk to you if you do.*

Hailey? He's here, isn't he? Hailey asked her who, knowing that she remembered her dad trying to kill her but testing her memory. *My father. He's in my office. I think he's going to kill me.*

No, he will never bother you again. On this, you can go to the bank. There was a moment of relief, then fear took its place. *You have to tell me what it is you're thinking, Ray. Your mind is going too fast for me to figure out.*

He hurt me, didn't he? Hailey told her that he'd hurt her badly before anyone could save her. *Yes, you told me that I had to scream, loudly, so that someone could come and save me. They did, didn't they?*

Yes. Danny, the local pack alpha, came with his men, but Alan had already hurt you badly. Danny killed your father to keep him from hurting you more.

Denny had told her that if she spoke to Ray in any way, she was to make sure she knew that she'd been hurt badly.

And to be honest with her when she asked how badly. Hailey didn't want to be responsible for telling her friend that she was more than likely going to be disfigured for the rest of her life, but she didn't want to lie to her either.

Ray, two things I want you to know right now. We have been keeping an eye on your places – home and business and even here. David is also with the local pack here. He's as safe as you are.

And the second thing? I'm calmer now, Hailey. I think I can take whatever it is you've been trying very hard for me to get on my own. How badly am I hurt? Hailey felt tears roll down her cheeks, and knew that it was now that she was going to have to be the one to hurt her friend. *Hailey? Tell me, please.*

Alan used a knife on your face. He cut you from cheek to ear. The doctors had to reattach it to your head, but Denny told me that you've not lost your hearing. Your lips have been busted up, as well as your eyes. The socket was busted all to fuck on the left, and your other eye is swollen too badly for them to know the damage there. She paused when Ray asked her to. *I want you to know that I love you very much, Ray. And think of you as my only sister.*

I love you too, Hailey. I felt that way the moment that you stood beside me that day. She could feel the sorrow in her voice, even if it was only in her head. *The rest, please. My arm feels heavy, so I'm assuming that it was broken.*

Yes, in two places. They're waiting for you to be stronger before they go in and repair it with metal rods. Also, your left hand was shattered when your father – Ray said not to call him that. *All right. I can do that. When Alan crushed your hand in the floor with his heel. They don't know at this point, even if they go in and repair it, if you're going to have full use of it.*

There's more, isn't there? Wait for that, please. I know that you've been saving the worst for last. You have no idea how much

I appreciate that, but just wait. How is married life? Getting any better? Hailey told her that it was. *I'm so happy for you. After everything that you've told me, I was hoping that I'd be one of their mates. But I'm supposing that they'd not want a freak like me in their life.*

Stop that right now, damn it. And you still might be. I'm hoping as much as you are for it to happen. Hailey let out a slow breath. *The only thing keeping us from being true sisters is blood. And that matters very little to me. I love you just as if you were my sister. I've told you this before. Now, I'll hear no more talk about that. All right?*

Yes, Momma. They both laughed. *Hailey, fix me. I want you to do for me what Dane did for you. I know that you can do it.*

No, I don't think that's a good idea. Ray asked her why not. *I don't know. But this shit that I have, it's scary stuff, Ray. I'm only just getting used to some of it. The things that I can do are —*

I don't want to be a freak of nature, Hailey. She could feel her sorrow and her pain. The timer on the meds she was getting automatically said she had about a minute to go before she'd be medicated again. *Never mind. You're right. Having all that juice, as you called it once, it could get me into more trouble than I usually am.*

The laughter from Ray was harsh and almost bitter. Before she could talk to her more, the meds kicked into her system and Ray was gone from her touch. Hailey could still read and feel her memories and pain level, which was lower now, but there wouldn't be any more conversation for a little while.

Getting up, Hailey went to the window. They'd brought Ray home as soon as she was cleared to go. She'd have to go to the hearing sometime soon — her father was still going to be charged with attempted murder.

9

Hailey watched the gardener fussing with the little herb garden that the cook had asked to have put in. It was just after Saint Paddy's Day, and things were starting to warm up. Just last week while out running with Colton, she'd seen crocus and daffodils coming up. Today there were blooms on the strawberries that Ken, the nice man that worked for Levi, had planted for the households. The man was doing great after his brain surgery.

It was little things, she knew, that would make her smile. In the last few weeks, things in her life had begun to shape up and be happy. At the beginning of her stay here with Colton, and then her recent marriage to the man, Hailey was trying to find one thing every day that she had to be grateful for. Life, she knew, had a way of changing when you least expected it to.

Sitting down again, she started reading some of the homework she should be grading. Hailey, unlike a lot of teachers where she worked, loved her job a great deal. And the kids seemed to be having a good time in her classes, too.

~*~

Levi looked around the room again. He'd been staying at a lovely bed and breakfast for the last two weeks, wanting to try things that he'd never done before after a show. While he knew that he'd done well at the show, he wouldn't know how well until he was home. He didn't want to think about anything but having fun, as Hailey had asked him to do.

Smiling, he thought of her asking him to have fun, and knew that it had been a direct order from her. She was adorable when she got all mother hen like, and he loved that she was a part of the family. Hailey could be all soft and mushy seeing a puppy on the television, but she'd also be the one that could cut a person to ribbons if anyone dared fuck with her family. Which, thankfully, he was a part of.

Going to the limo that was to take him to the airport, he thought of the conversation that he'd had with his brother last night. The woman, Ray Spencer, was healing well, but the outlook for her life wasn't good. She was depressed.

Levi knew this from talking to Hailey. He also knew that Ray had asked for Hailey to change her into what she was. Hailey wanted to—she'd told Levi that—but she was also afraid. What if she didn't get enough, or got too much of her blood and died? Levi thought about the question she'd asked him.

"If she turns out to be your mate—and I haven't any idea if she is or not—would you want me to change her?" He'd thought about that hard, but before he could come up with an answer, if he ever was to reach one, she spoke again. "As it stands right now, she will have to walk with a cane for the rest of her life. Her left hand will never hold another pencil or camera, nor will she be able to carry a child within her womb without it killing Ray or both of them. I just don't know what to do."

"I don't either, Hail. I mean, I guess I'd have to know for sure that is something that she could live with. The consequences. As for me telling you that you should do it, even if she turns out to be my mate that answer doesn't lay at my feet. It's her body, her life, and even her choice. You know that too." She said that she did, but was confused about it. "I am as well. I don't know what to tell you, love. You and her, you'll have to work that out. Or you could ask Dane."

She huffed at him. "You know as well as I do that Dane would have done it permission or not. She did the same

11

damned thing to me." They both laughed. "I think I will talk to Dane, however. Maybe this is all for nothing, and I can't change her into anything. I'm a copy of someone, not the original."

Now that he was headed home—he'd be there tomorrow afternoon—he thought of nothing else. Not of her injuries—he knew them to be extensive—but of the woman being his mate. Levi already knew a great deal about Ray, and thought that she was a great deal like Hailey. But he knew too that it could only be him hoping that she was a cuddly as her, and she might be an absolute terror. Not likely, but he didn't know.

He landed in New York as a stopover. All of a sudden, he didn't want to go home. Not that he was afraid of her—no, it wasn't that. But the unknown, about her being his mate, frightened him more than he wanted to admit. Levi knew just what sort of person he was—a slob that liked this his way.

"Dr. Stanton?" He looked up when someone said his name. His title wasn't something that a great many people knew about, and fewer knew that he was an artist. Nodding at the man, he said that was his name. "I'm Lucas Young. I work with Young and Young Attorneys. May I have a few minutes of your time?"

"No, I'm getting ready to catch a flight." He didn't tell him which one, nor where he was going when he asked. "What do you want? We can talk here."

Lucas looked around then back at him. Levi looked too, but kept his eye on the man. Backing up a little, he knew that he was in trouble when someone put their hands on his shoulders and held him tightly.

"You just had to make this more difficult, didn't you? I

said that you'd be hard, but no, the boss, he told me that you'd be a pussy." Levi reached for his family, every one of them, to tell them what was going on. Lucas, or whatever his name was, kept talking about his boss when Dane answered him.

I'm close to you, Levi. In the same store. Don't look for me. I've got your back. He was never so happy to hear that she was close to him in his life. *I've been following this fucking shit for two days. You have Hailey to thank for this, by the way. She and that thread thing, that's —*

Dane, I don't suppose we can talk about this later, can we? This shithole has a gun in my belly. And the one behind me is trying his best to tear my shoulders from my body. She laughed, and he could have gladly strangled her. He wouldn't, of course — she'd hurt him — but her laughter did ease his mind a great deal.

When I tell you to move, I want you to do it. Just tuck your head into the chest of the man behind you. I'll take care of the rest. She laughed again. *You do have something else to wear home, don't you?*

He asked her why just as she told him to tuck. And when he did, he felt the warmth of blood splatter down his neck to his chin. Lucas fell back, but had a knife in his hand that scared Levi as well. Levi just stood there until someone touched his arm. It was Dane.

"Come on, you're okay."

She had to drag him away from the crime scene. When he looked back as they hid behind a magazine rack, she could see that the shorter man, Lucas, was sitting up with a blade in his hand now, and Shoulder Man's head was lying in his lap.

Levi looked at Dane. "You killed him." She said that was what the plan had been. "And what about me? Why did you

13

drag me away?"

"So you don't have to miss your flight home, dummy." He would gladly have hit her if she wasn't dragging him to the back of the store they were in. "I have you something else to put on. It's not as fancy as your suit, but it'll get you home. There is—"

"I'm going to be sick."

She paused in her dialogue to let him throw up several times in the trash can that was suddenly there. As she stood there, she pulled out a phone and started talking, like the person had been waiting for her to call. He supposed, in a way, they had been once he heard her end of the conversation.

"It's done. And you will have to pick up the tab for a suit for my brother." A pause in the conversation had him standing up and glaring at her. "I have to go. My brother has puke on his chin, and I have to get him home to his mommy."

"That wasn't nice." She grinned. "You're not nice. I know you've been told that before, but I think, after what just happened, that I should be able to tell you that again. You are not a nice person."

"I saved your ass. And I'll tell you all about it once you change and we get on the other flight home. By the way, you do have puke on your chin." He wiped it off on his sleeve and saw that there was a great deal of blood there. "Don't. Just don't ask me now, all right? You're safe, and now that we're headed home, the rest of us can keep an eye on you as well."

He didn't ask her, even though he was burning with the need to know. This person, whoever it was, they were going to kill him. He didn't know that for sure, but he could feel it all the way to his bones. Sitting in his seat in first class, which he knew for sure his ticket hadn't been for, he glared at Dane when she asked the stewardess if she could have something to drink almost as soon as they were in the air.

"Here, you're to take these." He asked her what they are. "I want you to be able to listen to me with a clear head. Right now, I can tell that you're pissed off, and that you're in need to ask the million and one questions that are going on in your head."

Levi took them, then settled back in his seat. He should have made her tell him what he was taking, but honestly, he was so freaked out that he might have drank an entire bottle of liquor if she had handed it to him.

"They weren't after you." He'd never thought of that. All of his brothers had PhDs, so it could have been any one of them. "They thought they were getting Brayden. Because of me. But mostly because of the things that had been going on in Africa before he left."

"The thing with the donations and the houses." She nodded and smiled at him. "I don't understand. I thought that was taken care of months ago. Didn't someone go to jail over that? Not to mention, I think that they even told Brayden he was in the clear."

"They did. And he is. But that doesn't mean that the people who had to pay out the ass for stealing in the first place were happy." He asked her why they had to wait until now to tell him. "Because that's not all of it. And I need you to think very hard about what I'm about to tell you. Do you remember a man by the name of Roberto Perez? He would have talked to you at the show two weeks ago."

He closed his eyes, and he wasn't at all surprised to feel Hailey there. After telling him to wait for her, she moved through his mind gently and found the man for him. He

15

allowed it—he told himself it was because he was just too overwhelmed by this entire thing.

"Perez wanted me to paint his wife, or something like that, in the nude at his home. I told him that I didn't do that, not with a model, and that I had a timeline of things that I was working on anyway. He didn't seem too happy about it, but he did walk away." Before he could open his eyes, Hailey showed him the rest of the man's movement through the showing. "This is freaky, isn't it? I mean, it's like having a behind the scenes sort of camera following you around."

"She's good, and she has your back. But when she pauses, you listen to the conversation he has with this other man." Hailey followed the man through the rest of the time he was at the showing. Then when the man was leaving, he pulled out his phone and called someone. "Hailey has that number, so don't worry with it."

It hadn't even occurred to him to do that when the other man spoke. "Did you get him to do it?" Perez said that he hadn't. "Why the fuck not? My money not good enough for the fucker? You know what it is. He's a fucking gay, isn't he? That's why he's turning you down."

"I don't know, sir, but I couldn't get him to do it. He said something about having enough work on his timeline or something. I can try again." The man on the other end said that he'd take care of the little fucker—meaning him, Levi was sure. "All right then. There is no reason for me to come to the rest of the showing. I'll be home in two days, sir. After I arrive, we can work on something else to get him to your home."

"What does he want?" Hailey said that she didn't know. Even Dane, who could find a mole in a valley of tunnels, said she didn't know either. Without knowledge of the man on the other end, she hadn't any clue. "But you do think that it's more than just me painting his wife? And just so we're clear, whose wife is he talking about?"

"That is what threw us both at the start, too. Lucas said his wife, and then the other man says his wife. I'm not sure. Perhaps they're both lying, or they could really want you to paint their wives. Maybe together or some shit like that." Levi didn't comment. He had to think about whether Perez had come to the show on the second day. When he was sure that he'd not, he wondered what the hell was going on, and why him.

Sure, he could paint, but who would go to that much trouble for him to paint their spouse in the nude? And for that matter, why did he have to go to their home? Most painters he knew would say no to that. It was going to be a short flight, but Levi had a great deal on his mind to sort through. And most importantly, to see if Miss Spencer was his mate.

Chapter 2

Ray wasn't able to take any of the bandages off her face, not for a while yet, but she could hear just about anything that was around her. There was a bug of some sort buzzing against the screen to the window that was open. She supposed he wanted out. There were smells too.

Smiling, she heard someone in the gardens below her talking. She knew that he was alone, but he certainly wasn't happy with the way things were going with the planting he was doing.

Ray knew that he was planting something—roses, she thought. The smell of freshly turned soil hit her nose almost as soon as the window had been opened for her. Then the delivery man, someone that she knew wasn't the other man, had said he had the roses with him. The sound of them being offloaded was loud, so there must have been a great many roses being planted today.

"Dag nabbit, woman, why do you have to make this so hard on an old man? Just follow my diagram, she says. It's easy to read." He huffed. "I'm a doctor, not a gardener. And it don't matter a hill of beans if it means more to you if I plant them for you, when I have to have my hands all wrapped up from the blisters. Now does it?"

The door opened below her and she heard a woman's voice asking if Denny, she knew that name, wanted anything to drink. When he said he did and asked if he could sit down with her to drink it, Ray laughed at the woman's answer. She figured that the woman was his wife, and that she was a ball buster like Dane was.

"No. I want you to dig up the holes with one hand and drink your tea with the other, and not sit down on the job. What sort of person do you think I am, you old poop? I should bury you back here, but you being fertilizer might damage the roses Brayden got for me." She growled at him. "You are the most cantankerous old man I've ever met."

"But you love me." She giggled then, and Ray couldn't wait to meet them. To see the people who had been kind enough to take her and her little brother David in under such circumstances.

Everyone had been in and out of her room, she knew, at some point. But she couldn't speak to them yet. She had only just found out that she'd had her jaws wired together to prevent more teeth from being lost. She had lost all four of her front teeth, two up and two down, so she really wasn't in the mood to talk to anyone anyway. Better yet, for anyone to see her.

"Hello." She didn't know the voice, so she felt her body stiffen up with fear. "I'm Levi Stanton. You've not met me yet. I've been in France. I know from Hailey that you can't talk to me yet, so I'm waiting on her to come in here with us.

I'm truly sorry about all your pain and suffering, Ray. I am."

She knew what this man was in here for. Hailey had explained how the mates part worked, and they wanted to figure out if he was hers. Or something like that. Waiting, her fear of however this turned out was making her hurt. So when her hand was picked up and put into a much larger one, she moaned.

"I'm sorry, did I hurt you?" He rubbed her hand with his warmer one. "I'm a lot bigger than you are. Hailey told me that you're aware of what I am. A cougar. I'm a person too. I'm a man. Christ, I'm fucking this all up. Can I start all over?"

"You're a dork." She felt her mood lighten when she heard Hailey's voice. "I told you all you had to do was nip her a bit and you could speak to her. Why do you need me here when this might be private?"

"Because I'm sure that would go over well. 'Hello. I'm Levi, and pardon me while I add more pain to your poor abused body. I need to bite you a little so that I can have a conversation with you. Also, I might be your mate.'" She asked if he was. "I don't know. All I can smell is medicine and those damned roses that Dad is.... Hailey, just ask her if I can take a little of her blood, please?"

Ray wished she could have spoken to him. He was funny and flustered. She was sort of glad for that too. It made him seem less godlike and more human. She didn't know if she'd actually speak to him, but she'd love to see his face. She had yet to see any of their faces.

"She wants me to heal her." Ray jerked her hand from Levi when Hailey spoke, but Levi took it back into his and held her. "I don't know what to do. I want her up and around and like us, but I don't want to do something that she might

21

regret."

I won't. She spoke to Hailey. *And tell Levi that he should go now, before he does find out if I'm his mate and he's stuck with me. I'm not going to be anyone that could be seen with him.*

Hailey told Levi what she'd said, and Ray heard the door shut again. She waited for someone to speak, to tell her what was going on. Ray could feel her heart pounding hard and tried to calm herself. She would pay for it later if she didn't.

"Hailey left when I asked her to." Ray hadn't heard that, but didn't care. He really needed to get going. "If you'd rather I didn't bite you, then you only have to pull your hand from mine. I promise you, it won't be nearly as painful as I'm sure you've been through."

She didn't want to be alone. That was what she told herself when she didn't take her hand from his. And when Ray felt his breath on her wrist, she held herself stiff, waiting for the pain. When he licked her skin, it was all she could do not to moan. Then there was a small nip at her skin and Levi spoke again.

You're my mate. She waited for him to say something more, something about her not being right for him. With all the damage that had been done to her, he'd rather not be settled with her. But he said neither of those things. *I'm glad, if you want to know the truth. I've been thinking about it since I spoke to Hailey a few weeks ago. I wanted to come home then and figure it out. But I had obligations there, and a promise that I made to Hailey to fulfill. Which I have to tell you, she was right about. I won't tell her that, however.*

She has a big head already. They both laughed. *I can hear you speaking to me when you do. You don't have to use this mind thing if you'd rather not.*

22

"All right. As I said, you're my mate. And while I was away, I also thought about if you'd be healed by either of my sisters. And they're my sisters, despite being married into the family. As I'm sure you'll be once we are married. If you want to marry me, that is. I'm a slob."

I heard. He didn't say anything, but she could almost feel his humor. *I hate to admit it, but I've never seen your work. I've heard about it a great deal. Do you want them to make me better looking?*

"I know what you looked like before. I don't now, of course, but you are going to be beautiful to me, no matter the scars. But this isn't a decision that I can make for you. I will support you, in any way that you want. Like you having a child or not—this is your body and your decision." She told him that she couldn't have children. "I heard about that as well. And if you decide not to have one of them give you their blood, that's all right as well. There are plenty of children out there that need a good home. My brother and his wife, they have three little girls—two they adopted, and one on the way. He's a boy, however. If you don't mind, though, I'd like to have a little more practice before we do that."

Ray was charmed by him. He told her about his show; how many paintings he'd sold—all of them—and what he'd done before coming home. Hailey had told him to relax and have fun.

She was forever telling me to do that too. But then this came along, and now I'm bored out of my mind. I can't even read anything now that I have time. Ray moved a little, just to give her back some relief, and she cried out in her mind. *I'm so sick of this bed too. I don't think I ever want to sleep in it again.*

Levi laughed. "Yes, well, until recently I didn't even have

a bed at my place. I had a nice sleeping bag that I used at home. Don't ask me why I did that when I could well afford one. But I do have a cot in the studio where I work. And soon, I'm going to be moving into a building downtown. Just so I can have a nice window to look out of." She asked him where he lived. "Nearby here. You're at my parents', in the event you didn't know. I live right across the street from them. All of us have purchased homes close to them. We're a very tight family."

Hailey said you guys are afraid of your mom. Are you? He said he was. They all were. *I heard them today, out in the back yard. Your father was planting roses for your mom. It sounds like she has a great many of them to put in the ground.*

"Several months ago, my oldest brother, Brayden, came home from Africa and had a woman with him. She was Vonda. Have you heard about her?" She told him that she'd not. "Well, there was a loony person. No, that's much too gentle. She was off her fucking rocker. Anyway, one night in a fit of rage, she went to the garden and destroyed all of my mother's roses—ones that she had been nurturing for decades. And she had some prize winners back there too. Brayden felt so bad about it that he and Dad took her to the nursery in town and got her whatever she wanted. Mom was pissed off, as you can well imagine. But now she gets to start fresh and put them in by design, rather than just wherever she plopped them down in the dirt."

The two of them talked for a long time. She had no idea how much time had passed, but she was enjoying herself. And when she was starting to be in pain—which happened less and less of late, but it still hurt her—he told her that he'd read to her while she rested, and left her to get a book. Levi

24

told her that there was a huge library here and he'd be back.

Before he came back, Dane came to speak to her.

"Hailey told me what you want. And if you really want it, I can do that for you. She said that she would have, but since we didn't know what happened to her when she took my blood, Hailey thinks you should get it from the well and not the cup. Are you all right with that?" Ray could talk to Dane too, but no one else in the house. She told her that she was more than all right with it. "But I want you to think about it a great deal, Ray. Anything and everything could happen. You might just be able to heal yourself or not. I haven't any idea. All right?"

Yes. I understand. But trying is better than me wondering, don't you think? And please don't tell anyone yet. I don't know what Levi wishes to do yet, but I guess I'm his mate. Dane told her that was wonderful. *I don't know yet. We're only just talking to each other. The two of us might hate one another once I'm better. If I get better, that is.*

"Doubtful that he'd care what you looked like. The Stanton men, they're the best you could ever hope for in a spouse. Not to mention, they're the kindest, most gentle men you'll ever meet. Just like their parents." Ray didn't answer her. She didn't know anyone, not really, except for Hailey. "And all Hailey can talk about is how much you and her have hit it off, right from the start."

She's like the sister I never had. Dane took her hand in hers and gave it a tight squeeze. *I want to do this, Dane. I need to do this. I've been thinking about it for several days. My father did this to me, and would have killed me. If I just hide away, hang my head in shame, then I feel as if he won.*

"What is it you think you will lose if you don't have me

try this?" Ray didn't know how to explain it well, but did the best that she could. "All right. *That* I can get behind. Yes, I would guess that you would hide, not just what you look like, but your work too. It would be a shame, after all you've done to make your furniture a household name, to have someone take it all from you this way. Your father, one way or the other, he would have won if he could make you quit what you love doing—by death or by you just becoming a hermit. I want you to talk to Levi too. He won't decide for you, that much I know for sure, but he will help you with whatever happens. All right?"

She said that she would, and thanked her. Dane told her not to thank her yet—for all she knew, this might be nothing at all. Ray didn't believe that. No more than she thought that Levi would ever harm her. And that, she thought, was something that she had been afraid of most. Someone that hurt her all the time.

Chapter 3

Levi walked through his home when he returned there after supper. He'd enjoyed being with his family. It had been so much fun, because he knew that he was more relaxed than he'd been in a long while. He knew it had a great deal to do with Ray, but the family all thought that it was because he'd taken that trip with his brothers, and then taken a few extra days in France to have a look around.

He needed more furniture. That much was obvious to him as soon as he entered his living room. There wasn't even a painting on the wall in this room. Nor had he ever invested in a television set or wood for the fireplace. It wasn't until he was standing next to it that he realized that it was gas operated and not a wood burner. Laughing at himself, he went to the kitchen. There was the heart of his home.

"You do know that she designs furniture, don't you? And it's not at all what I thought it was." Barnes, his cook, handed him a catalog that looked as if it had seen better days. "I can tell you for a fact that it's well made, and works just the way it says that it will. I bought the bedroom suite on page twenty-seven a few years ago, and it still looks as good as the day it was delivered."

Levi opened the catalog to the first page and whistled. "This is beautiful. I don't know why, but I had it in my head that it was all steel and chrome. But it's all wood based things. I love this dining room table. It looks a great deal like the one that Colton just got." As he flipped through the pages, Barnes handed him a pen and he began marking the things that he liked. "Do you think I could get a discount? She's my mate, did I tell you?"

The pop to the back of his head had him turning to look at the older man. His glare might have scared another person, but Levi knew that he was a pussy cat. Levi asked him what that was for.

"You have a mate. I'm betting, since I've not heard about it in town, that you didn't tell your father as yet either, did you?" He said that he wanted to hold it to himself for a few more days. "I can understand that, but you really need to share this with them. You know how they can.... Never mind what I said. You're right. I know how they can be, and you need to hold this to you. Yes, smart man. But I don't want to be there when you finally do tell them. Your mother will hit you harder than I did."

"She will. But I'm enjoying getting to know Ray. That's what she likes to be called. Her name is Rachel Spencer. I read to her this evening so that she could hear something other than my parents bickering about the roses." They both laughed. "She's sweet, but I have a feeling that she can be like the rest of them when necessary. She wants Dane to give her some of her magical blood so that she can heal. I think it has more to do with the scars she has than healing, but that's going to be her decision. Not mine."

He didn't care what her reasons were for doing it. He wanted her to be happy. Levi thought that if she didn't do this, she'd never leave the house. Not that she was vain or anything like that, but Hailey had told her the extent of the injuries that she'd had to her face. And all from her father.

"Barnes, what do you know about what happened to Ray? I have read the little bit in the paper about her father coming to her office. There really wasn't much said in the paper where I was." Barnes sat down after getting a thick envelope from the cabinet. "You've been saving them for me?"

"No. Not you in particular. But for you or Wyatt. In actuality, I had hoped that she'd be your mate. But in the event that she was your brother's, I thought it best to be prepared. If there are gaps in the information, I'm afraid that is due to Ms. Dane. She was trying to keep as much out of the paper as she could, in the event that it drew the aunt here quicker. Did she tell you that she thinks that she will come here?" Levi nodded. "I've not met the woman, but from what young David tells us, she is a horror. Much worse than her brother."

Levi found that hard to believe, but he didn't know. So picking up the newspaper clippings, he made his way back to the bedroom. He decided, however, to take a nice shower. He'd been sitting here for two days, and he was sure that he stank.

The water was much nicer than he remembered. The B&B that he had stayed in had plenty of water and it was hot, but it was hard, making it difficult to soap up or even to wash his hair. But here, he knew that the house had a whole house softer, and he moaned when he was able to wash up and clean off so nicely. He even shaved and put on cologne, something that he rarely did anymore. He wanted to smell nice for Ray. Levi laughed at himself as he made his way back to his chair.

They were laid out in order of date. He read the first one, and was surprised to find out that it wasn't about the attempted murder, but about the woman in his bed. Yesterday they'd had her moved to his home, where there were people there all the time. Levi honestly just wanted her to be in their home.

Ray had won a great many awards with her designs that blended nicely with the antiques that she had collected over the years. It did mention her great grandma, and Levi took a moment before reading on to remember the elderly lady and the fun they'd had with her.

What has you happy? He smiled when Ray spoke to him. He told her what he'd been thinking about. *Yes, David told me about it. He said that he wished all the time that he'd gone with you guys. But he was afraid of Alan finding out and hurting them both. He would have, too.*

"I'm sure, now that I know a little about it, that he would have. I've been looking over your catalog. Our butler, Barnes, has some of your pieces, he told me this morning." She asked him which ones. "He said that he has a bedroom suite, and that it looks as good now as when he bought it. I was thinking that we need to get something for this house. The bed that you're sleeping in is mine, but it's only a single. And the only other things that I have are some of the pieces that I picked up at auctions."

He could tell that she was trying to think hard on something, so he let her. He didn't want her to be hurt. Levi had realized that he already loved her, but he also was a little afraid for her. Not with the aunt—Levi was sure that they could protect her from her—but how she would feel about him telling her how much he already loved her.

I have some pieces too. Those are in storage, as I have...had only a small apartment where I worked. But Grandma, she gave me quite a few pieces that, as I said, are in storage. Are you expecting me to live here with you? Levi asked her what she wanted to do. *I've no idea. It's not like I know what is going on around me most of the time. I just feel overwhelmed by everything.*

"I can understand that. Your inability to see, I would imagine that is knocking everything out of perspective for you. But, you'll be happy to know that I spoke to my dad, and he said that I could take you outside if you wanted to go. There is—"

Oh yes, please. He laughed, and asked her if she'd like to go now. *Yes. I never had much time to be in the sunshine before. I was working too much, I know that now. And I need to call my business. They know that I was in the hospital, but I should make sure they know what's going on. Can you read to me out there as well?*

"Anything you want, my dear." She had lost weight even since him bringing her to his home the other day. "I'll have Barnes take out a blanket and lay it over the chair I have in mind. That way, if you are chilled, you can wrap up in it."

Reaching to his friend, he told Barnes what they were doing. The man was happy to help, and said that he'd serve them both a nice snack while he was with her. Before he got her picked up and down the stairs, he knew that Barnes would make it happen.

The sun was shining off the pool that had been uncovered to be cleaned. A couple of days ago he'd had the yard given

31

a good once over and the pool house fixed up for guests. He thought it was very beautiful back here, and had agreed with the person who did his lawn to have some spring flowers put in, as well as a couple of bushes that would brighten up the yard.

"There you go. Now, I'm going to give you a view of the yard so you can tell where things are. Also, not that I want you to walk, but the doors to the house are just to your right. Barnes also brought out a baby monitor so that he can hear us when we're out here." He went over the entire yard for her, including all the things he was going to have done to it, if she approved. "Tonight, if you're up for it, we'll even grill out. All right?"

I so love burgers on the grill. I've not had a homemade burger in ages. With potato salad and chips. Pickles — I love lots of pickles too. She laughed in his head. *Oh my, I don't even know how I'm to eat it, but if you do and let me smell it, I'll be almost in heaven.*

He was just picking up the book he was reading to her, still laughing, when Dane came to talk to him. He could tell by the look on her face that whatever she had to tell him, it was not going to be happy news. She asked Ray how she was feeling.

I'm fine. Get to it. They both laughed. *She's coming, isn't she? My aunt. And you're either telling me that you're going to send me away, or that you're getting the wagons in a circle.*

"Both. But I have a few things that I would like for the two of you to do before she gets on a plane to come here. She's out for David most of all, and she'll demand some of her mother's things too. Hailey told me that she's been notified of both her mother and brother's deaths, and the will is to be read in ten days. I've delayed it as much as I could. You two need to get married." Ray didn't say anything, and neither did he. They were still getting to know each other. "Also, the paperwork for you both to adopt David as your son is filled out. I only need for you to sign off—"

You're thinking that this will stop her? Levi waited for Dane to answer Ray. *It won't, let me tell you that much.*

"No, I don't think it will, but it will slow her down in trying to get what she wants. And right now, the more we can delay her from leaving here with anything, the better it will be for me finding things on her. I cannot find a thing that says that she was a biological sister to Alan at all." Ray said that she had Grandma's Bible, but it was in her storage locker. "If you don't mind, I can bring your things here and get the Bible in a couple of hours. If you okay that."

All right. But I have some questions. Why does it matter if we're married? Dane told her. *I see. Me being temporarily blind could make it so that I'm unfit. All right. So he's my husband and can care for David while I can't at the moment. And the adoption?*

"You, according to my paperwork, adopted him the day after you had custody of David. All I need is for you to sign off on it and it'll be filed on the right date and marked that way. You and Levi marrying also gives him the opportunity to adopt him so that he has a real family, as in mother and father figures that will care for him. The wedding will be dated two weeks ago, the adoption will be a couple of days ago. The date that the application was filed is going to be the day after you were wed, just to cover our asses. I'll have the dates all lined up for you to know." Levi asked if they were going to do it soon. "Right now, if you're up for it. I know this isn't what anyone wants. Lucy is about to have a kitten. But it's what we need to do to keep you all together."

Levi looked at Ray. She was thinking hard, he thought. Either that or she was holding onto her temper. She had only just told him that she was overwhelmed, and now there was this hitting them. Reaching for her hand, he told her he was sorry.

I am too. I was hoping that we could get to know each other a little more. But I guess this will be all right. What about getting me well enough to fight this fucking cunt? Because, as I'm sure you've figured out, Aunt Caroline has the personality of a flea-bitten mule, as my grandma used to say. They all laughed, then the minister stepped out of the house to marry them. *I'm profoundly glad that he couldn't hear me.*

Levi laughed. It was funny, really, that they all could have a conversation with Ray and no one could hear her. He just realized that he'd never heard her voice, had never seen her face nor her smile, and he wanted that more than anything. Levi wasn't even going to be able to kiss his bride properly. But then he realized that might be all right too. He really would overwhelm her if he did that.

So, in a very short order, the paperwork was signed off on and he became a father to David. David was happy; the kid looked like he might have had his birthday and Christmas wishes all fulfilled. When his entire family arrived, he was married. In less time than it took him to eat a sub, he was not only married, but a dad too. Levi loved every second of it.

~*~

Caroline Spencer was trying her very best to make sure that she didn't lose her temper. Normally she would have had someone drive her to the courthouse to have the wills read to her, but today she was having an off day, a day when she was pinching her pennies and didn't have any staff.

34

Usually that didn't bother her or interfere with her day. But her brother had died, and her mother almost a week earlier. She wasn't terribly upset about her mother — she hadn't ever liked her in the first place. But Alan, he was her buddy. The one that she could count on — usually. When he got poor — well, he wasn't fit to be around anymore.

She'd not spoken to him in years because he was forever tight on money. She had told him, several times when he was younger, that he needed to save his money and put some away for a rainy day. To him, it was pouring every day, she thought. And after giving him money once and finding out that he was betting it on cock fights, of all things, she had cut him off.

Rachel. Every time she thought of that child, she wanted to lean over and puke her belly up. It wasn't that she was ugly, no. Rachel had turned out to be quite the looker. But she was just like her mother. Into things that didn't concern her, and then treating her father like a turd. Caroline had thought him one herself, but she hadn't taken him to raise like Rachel had. Daughters needed to care for their fathers.

Her mother, Alma Spencer, hadn't been a bad parent, but she was a hillbilly. She even thought it was cute of her to be able to make her own corn meal, and to make that nasty corn bread pudding for her. Caroline didn't like anything *homemade*. Nor did she eat things that had been *cured* in a smokehouse. That stuff would just get you killed.

Once, about fifteen years ago, she'd gone to visit her mother. She was living alone then — eating off the land, she called it. And when she entered the house, Caroline nearly did puke on the floor because her mother was cooking collared green and turnips. Something even to this day Caroline didn't like.

"Don't turn your nose up at my dinner, Carol. You used to eat this all the time when you were perching your butt right there on that chair. Why, I even think you might have gotten yourself seconds, or more." Caroline told her mother that she ate civilized food now. "You think we're so different, daughter? Why, we're just two cheeks of the same arse, you know."

It was crap like that that had her moving as far away as she'd been able to when she'd gotten out of school, and she hadn't returned. Caroline had even told her mother that nothing would bring her back there but her death.

Smiling to herself, Caroline wondered what the old place looked like now. Whatever it was, she was going to empty it of the jewelry and other things that might bring her a few dollars, then she was going to have the house burnt to the ground with all that antique crap in it.

The first thing she'd bought herself when she got some money was modern things. Chrome and glass. Not that she cared all that much for it either, but it wasn't a dining room table that some old fart had made that had been used as a birthing table, or even for laying out the dead. Caroline shivered when she thought of how many meals she'd eaten where a nasty child had been brought into the world.

David was hers now, she knew that. And she was going to make sure she raised him to be just like his father. He'd been frightful with money, yes, but he'd been a good man otherwise. No one ever saw that but her. The only thing she'd do different with David, her nephew, was teach him the meaning of money. He'd learn it her way or she'd beat it into him. In fact, she thought as she pulled into the handicapped parking place, she might just start that way. He had been living with her mother all this time.

As soon as she got out of her car, someone pointed out that she didn't have a handicapped placard. Ignoring him for getting into her appointment, she thought that since she paid the city taxes, she could just park wherever it was convenient for her. People were just too overly sensitive anymore.

Mr. Russel Butler was the attorney that had called her about her brother. She had known that her mother was dead, and good riddance to her. Caroline knew that her mother wouldn't have left her anything. But she would have to her dear son. Although she knew that Mother wasn't all that keen on giving Alan anything while she was living, who else would she leave it to but him?

Having a seat where she was supposed to, she waited on Mr. Butler.

"I'm going to read your mother's will for you now. Since she was the first to pass on, this way you'll know what was left to whom so that you can figure out your part in this after I read your brother's will. All right?"

"Yes, of course. But just skip to the part of my brother's and my things. I don't want to have to sit here and listen to you drone on about what sort of person she was. I know. She was my mother, after all."

"Yes, all right."

He asked if she would like some refreshments.

"Unless it says that I can have something in that will from you, then I don't want to talk about anything else. Read the wills."

He read that she was to receive all her mother's canned goods. Canned goods? She asked him what that meant. Did he mean things that were from the store?

"No. I believe she left you all the jars of fruit and vegetables that she put up from her own garden. There are also packages of seeds that she left you. And her comment on it was, she didn't want you to starve if there was ever a zombie uprising." Butler laughed, but Caroline didn't find any humor in it. "I'll continue."

Alan wasn't to get anything. He had taken all that he wanted when he'd robbed her two years ago. Butler told her that would have been two years, as the will was only just updated last month.

"Alan was to have a list of things that he stole from her, their value, as well as everything that he destroyed when he went on a rampage once while she was canning tomatoes." Butler looked at her and she just waved him on. "Rachel Spencer is to get everything else, including the contents of the house, that didn't sell as well as the Ford. David has his share in the bank for college."

"What about the land? She doesn't mention that." Butler looked through the paperwork and looked at her before speaking. "This is going to take a great deal longer if you don't just answer my questions when I ask them of you. Who gets the land?"

"Alma Spencer didn't own the land that the house set on. And upon her death, Rachel got the home and the contents as well, those that Alma didn't sell at the auction. Rachel Spencer has owned all six hundred acres for the last ten years, and received the house upon your mother's death. She is also claiming the seven companies that your mother sat on the board for, as well as all monies in the bank." She wanted to know how that came about, but he continued reading. "The household items not claimed by Rachel or David Spencer will be sold at auction in early March. The jewelry, too, is to be divided between the two of them to do with as they please. From what I understand, there was a great deal of it."

"When did she have an opportunity to wear it is what I would like to know. When she was feeding the chickens? Or perhaps when she out there making her own cheese that she milked from the cows?"

"I don't believe that cheese comes directly from the cows, Ms. Spencer." She slammed her hand down on the desk. "Yes. No information that you don't ask for."

He was laughing at her—she could see it on his face. But as he read the last of the will and handed her the seeds, Caroline simply dropped them in the trash. What on earth did her mother think she was going to do with seeds? Toss them at some dirt and hope they came up?

When he read over Alan's will, it was as if Mother and him had not spoken. He went on about how he had inherited all his mother's worldly goods, and that they were to go to Caroline. There was a mention of David, and if underage, he was also to go to his aunt. There was an account set up for him that Alan hadn't been able to touch—a million-dollar policy. It had been something from David's mother that was to go with him when he was sent to his aunt. She asked Butler about that.

"I'm sorry, but there isn't a policy from his mother that can be claimed by you. Or anyone for that matter." She asked him what he meant by that. "Well, Rachel, his sister, has full custody of David, and has moved the policy to her own bank. The courts gave her that—"

"What do you mean, Rachel has full custody of him? As

you just read to me, he's mine to take home with me. And that policy." Butler said something about the courts overriding what was in the will. "No they do not. I'm going to have to have someone get both that brat and that money for me. I don't need it, but Rachel isn't going to be using it either. I'll just see about that."

He was still talking as she made her way out the door. No one spoke to her, for which Caroline was glad. She would have removed heads in the mood she was in. Of all the nerve of that woman. Well, Caroline would take care of that soon enough.

There was a parking ticket on her car when she got there. Also, a man was hooking it up to his tow truck. She opened her car door while he was working to get under it, and not only drove over the sidewalk to get away from it, but also hit a street sign. Caroline would gladly have run over the man too, she was that angry. But that would have made her wait longer to get to Rachel and this trouble she was causing.

"Damn that girl. Well, we'll just see who is the smarter of the two of us. Money gets things done, and I'm better off than Rachael will ever be in two lifetimes."

She pulled into her driveway and went into her house. Packing was easy—Caroline didn't think she'd be there all that long. She'd have this mess cleared up in two days, or she'd not just lose her temper, but she'd make sure that Rachel was lying out beside her grandmother if she gave her any crap.

Chapter 4

"I want to tell you two things right off the bat here. When I helped Hailey, she was nearly dead. And I will admit now that I gave her too much. She's my friend, and I didn't want to lose her. Not that you aren't my friend too, but you're not dying." Dane let out a deep breath and something occurred to Levi. She was afraid. "Second...I forgot what that is. But that just makes the first one all that much more important, damn it. I don't want anything to fucking happen to you."

I know that. Levi took Ray's hand into his as they sat there. *I don't want anything to happen to me either. But I figure this is my best chance of being happy. Having a good life. Here with you guys. And Dane, you're my friend as well. All of you have come to mean a great deal to me. And I have no idea who you are.*

Dad wiped his face with his ever-present hankie and asked her if she was ready. When Ray said that she was, he injected something into her IV to put her to sleep. Dad didn't foresee any issues with taking the wires out of her jaws, but he didn't want to take the chance that something could go wrong. When she was asleep, everyone but him left the room.

"I don't want anything to happen to her, Levi. She's come to mean a great deal to me." He told his dad that he loved her too. "Yes, and I have to tell you, I've never seen you so relaxed before either."

"It's all because of her. And, believe it or not, I'm feeling like I can go back to my studio for a while as well." Levi grinned at his dad. "She's my mate too."

"I think we all figured that out, son." Dad didn't even look up from what he was doing. "You're happy and you're very relaxed. A mate can do that for you, especially when she comes to you at a time when you need her. And you did. Now, let me work. By the way, I'm telling your mom. She knows too, but expect some kind of punishment for making her wait for you to spill the beans."

He watched his dad work to remove the wires, then had to leave for a moment. It was hurting her, was all his cat could see. As he stepped out onto the patio that was just outside the offices, he drew in the smells surrounding him.

I'm headed in. Dane made him smile, as she sounded so unsure. *I hope, if nothing happens or too much happens, that both of you can forgive me.*

There will be nothing to forgive you for, Dane. If it works, then that's wonderful. If it doesn't, we're not out anything but a little blood. We will both love you very much for trying this. Even though we all know you're a little afraid. She snorted at him. *Well then, you tell me what you're apprehensive about.*

If you tell anyone this, I'll cut you up so badly that you'll look like — Holy fuck, Levi. She really is a mess. Did you want to come here before I help her? He said that he did not. He wanted no memories of what she looked like right now. *I don't blame you.*

And I'm hoping that she doesn't remember this either. Christ, if he wasn't already dead, I'd kill him myself.

He wanted to run—just become his cat and run through the woods. But he wanted to be there, just in case something didn't go right. Sitting on the deck chair, he thought about things that didn't have anything to do with the happenings going on just behind him.

There hadn't been any work that came back from the show in France. In fact, there had been a bidding war on two of them that had ended with him making more than double on each of the works. Levi was itching to get back to his work. It had been ages since he'd wanted to go into the studio for work that was even in progress.

His work was known as surrealism. The muse, or whatever it was called, that was the creative part of him would add different objects into a single work of art that would blend together so well that you'd have to look very hard to see all the different elements in the work.

Levi was known for that, as well as for his work in Chinese art. However, instead of signing those pieces with his first name, he used his initials, LJS, with his first name under it, to bring them all together. His painting of cougars lying on a bed of poppies was one of the paintings that had been in the war. Levi loved painting on silk. It was expensive, but the end result was magnificent.

It's working. He let out a breath that he'd been holding for a few seconds, and felt the weight of the last few weeks lift from his heart. Dane laughed as she continued speaking. *Christ, her front teeth that had been knocked out are there as well. You should come in now, Levi. She looks about three thousand percent better already.*

Going back into the offices, he watched as Dad took off the casts that had been on her leg and arm. He could see where her hand was already healed, the one that her father had crushed. Her face was still bad looking, but they were scars now instead of wounds. And as he watched, they began to disappear as well. Taking her hand into his, he kissed the back of it and sobbed like a small child.

"She'll be so happy." His dad patted him on the back and wiped the tears that he'd been shedding as well. "I've never seen her before this. I mean, I've seen pictures of her— What are you doing, Dane?"

"I have to give her a bit more, Levi. She might be healed, but I want to make sure that she can look in the mirror without cringing. Or worse yet, remembering what had been done to her." He watched as she dropped a few more bits of blood into her mouth. Then when she'd given her about ten more drops of her blood, Dane rubbed her cut finger over her scars. "I have to be sure that she is healed. She trusted me, Levi. From the very start, she trusted that I'd make her whole. That I'd make sure that she was ready to face the world. I cannot let her down. She means a great deal to me and the rest of us."

Levi sobbed. Since he'd known her, he had never thought that someone could touch Dane in this way. But whatever her blood had in it, it was working. The scars that were still forming were disappearing as Dane's blood was absorbed into Ray's flesh.

Dane and his dad both left after that. Dane was still crying, her heart breaking for his mate. Holding Ray's hand, he watched the wounds that had been so heinous heal. Ray's skin was glowing with good health. Dad had removed the IV before he left, and even that wound was gone. Kissing the

44

back of her hand again, he held it to his cheek as he spoke to her.

"You are so much more beautiful than I ever imagined you'd be." He laughed. "Not that I thought you'd be ugly, but I cannot believe how you simply take my breath away. When you're all better and stronger, I'm going to show you our home. I've been shopping for pieces that I think will go nicely with what I have. And anything that you don't care for, we can burn if you want."

"Why would you do that?" Her voice was like a long remembered melody to him. Kissing her on the mouth, he sat back down and smiled. He was sure that he looked like a loon. "No, just very happy. Hey, I'm talking. It must have worked."

"Yes." Overcome with emotion, he laid his head on her breast and watched her face. When her fingers moved through his hair, he closed his eyes. Levi's love for this woman was almost too much. But he knew that to tell her—words would never do it justice. "I love you. That seems so tame for how I feel, but you cannot believe how much I do."

"I love you as well, Levi. Do you think I could sit up?" He told her what his dad had told him, that she needed to move slowly. "Yes, I will. I don't want to fall on my ass after all of this. And I want a shower. A long hot one, so I can wash off all the smells I'm sure that I have."

"How about if we work up to that? For now, let's get you sat up and wait to see how you feel after that."

Ray swayed just a little when she was sitting up. And when he helped her put her feet over the side of the bed, she pulled her gown down.

"My legs haven't been shaved in ages." He laughed. Levi simply couldn't help it. It was funny, after all she'd been

45

through, for her to worry about something so mundane as her legs. "Well, to me it's a big deal. The first time I sleep with you, I want to be able to tell my legs from yours."

"I don't care if you have to braid it down your legs." She made a puking motion, and Levi laughed again. "I'll help you, if you let me take a bath with you. How about that?"

"Anything. And you know what? I'm starving. All I can think about is a burger. And French fries. Also, I don't ever want to drink a smoothie or a milk shake again. I'm done with soft foods altogether. Maybe mashed potatoes. I love those. Oh, and I want a piece of cherry pie. With ice cream. I know that is soft, but—"

Levi kissed her. Standing in front of her, he pulled her soft body to his and moaned when she wrapped her legs around his hips. When he pulled back, the hardest thing he'd ever done, he laid his head on hers and just took in her scent. Just about the time he was ready to profess his love for her again, her belly growled.

"I'm really hungry." Picking her up, he carried her down the stairs. She was still listing all the things that she wanted to eat, and Mom was getting things ready for her. When she sat a bowl of soup in front of Ray, she just looked at it, then his mom. "No offense, but I want something I can sink my teeth into. Something crunchy. Chips."

Ray got up and opened the cabinets. Mom just stayed out of her way, laughing the entire time. It was wonderful to see Ray up and around. And when she sat at the table, shoving the soup away, he watched her devour a bag of chips and some cookies.

"She never wants to eat something soft again." Ray nodded at Mom as he explained it to her. "Also, we're going to have burgers on the grill tonight. Why don't you all come over, and we'll have a wonderful evening in celebration of Ray being up and around. All right?"

"What a lovely idea. And I'll call up Barnes now and see what he needs help with. Oh yes, Levi, this is a good idea." She sat down with them, and he could tell that she was going to say something he didn't want to hear. But he didn't stop her. "You have no idea how very sorry I am that I demanded that you allow me to see into that room you have."

Levi had forgotten about it—it seemed so long ago. He wanted to tell her that it didn't matter, but it had. That was something that he'd wanted private. Something that was his and his alone.

"I didn't look." Levi looked at his mom, and wondered first if she was trying to make him feel better, or if she really had not looked. "I knew that I had hurt you. Just as soon as you walked away, I knew that even as a mother, I had overstepped my boundaries with you. But you've never let us in on your work. Never showed us anything that you've done. You haven't even let me have a piece that I can hang in my home so that I can brag on my little boy."

"I didn't know you wanted any." Not only did Mom pop him on the back of the head, but so did Ray. "Well, I didn't. Besides, it was something that I did that was private."

"Why?" Levi asked Ray what she meant. "Why is it private to your family, but not so much to the public? And honestly, I had no idea you were an artist. You knew who my grandma was, correct?" He nodded. "What do you think would have happened if she'd not put her work out there so that people could see it? Do you have any idea how many letters and cards I received when she passed away from people that had some of her work? And stories behind it. Those kept me going when it was the darkest for me. Grandma would give it away if someone didn't have the funds but enjoyed her work. So many times she would donate one of her pieces to a hospital or some kind of long term care facility to pay the bills for someone that was down on their luck."

"What do you think my family, mostly my brothers, would say if they saw them? They'd laugh at me." Two more pops to the back of the head. "You guys keep this up and I'm going to have a brain injury. I'll let you guys see them, but you two first. Then if you think you'd like for the rest of the family to see them, I can work up to that. And Mom, you get first choice of whatever pieces you wish. Anything out there, it's yours."

"Good. I'll take it all." She was laughing as she left, and Levi looked at Ray, who was still munching on her chips.

"Do you really think she'll take it all?" Ray kissed him, chip crumbs and all, then nodded. "Yeah, that's what I was afraid of. I might be out of business before the next show."

~*~

The drive was much harder than she thought it would be. Caroline didn't care for people, and especially stupid ones. But she was going to have to modify that soon. She didn't care for stupid people driving cars. And they were everywhere.

No one used their turn signals any more, she'd noticed. But they sure could lay on their horns when you did something to them. Twice now she'd had to pull over to the side of the road when the honking became too much for her. She wanted to get out, slap the snot out of them, and go on her way. But she didn't. Caroline had things to do, and bothering with these people today would have taken too long. At least that was the feeling she got from them. Driving along at ten miles over the speed limit, they would hang their big beefy arms out the window, and play their music so loud that it gave her a headache, even being two cars behind them.

Stopping for gas had been humiliating. Caroline didn't have any idea how to open the little doors that everyone seemed to have on their car, much less know how to put the gas in once she found it under the license plate. She noticed then, too, that the little number in the corner wasn't up to date — it was off by four years. Oh well, Caroline thought. She paid her taxes, and that was all they were getting out of her.

"Your plates are expired." She glared at the woman talking to her with a baby smashed up against her chest. "Your licenses plates. They're expired. If the police pull you over —"

"They'll get the boot end of my foot is what they're going to get. Mind your own business. I didn't tell you that you're smothering your baby, did I?" The woman huffed at her and said something about her being rude. To show her the real meaning of rude, she sprayed gas on her. "See? That's being rude. Too bad I don't have a lighter, or I'd show you extreme rudeness."

After paying for her gas, Caroline got into her car and drove off. More stupid people. Everywhere she went, they were coming out of the woodwork. Like the people at the restaurant she had stopped at.

"I'd like a large black coffee, no sugar, and a plain donut to go." That was just what she said to the woman.

Then Milly, her name tag said, came back with, "What sized coffee you want?"

"I'd like a large black coffee, no sugar, and a plain donut

to go."

Milly must have been one of those retarded people, because she looked her right in the eye and asked her if she wanted cream and sugar. Caroline couldn't help it, she reached over the counter to slap her and Milly backed up. Dang girl.

"Where is your manager? I demand to speak to someone in charge right now." The girl turned and looked at an equally stupid looking woman. "I told her exactly what I wanted — a large black coffee, no sugar, and a plain donut to go. And she insists in asking me stupid questions that I already answered. What is wrong with her? Besides being incompetent?"

"Ma'am, I'm going to have to ask you to lower your voice." Caroline felt her head pound, she was so angry. "Now, what is it you wanted? And I can get it for you. I heard coffee — what size did you want?"

She could not help it. Caroline swept her hands over the counter top and knocked everything on it to the floor. Donuts went flying. The coffeemaker hissed as it flew through the air and hit the table next to it. Milly and her manager were covered in red and brown goo. They looked as if they'd been pooped on. It was even hanging from Milly's chin.

Storming out of the place, no one tried to stop her. Caroline was so mad that all she could do was start the car, then turn it off. Anger made her fingers burn to go back in there and teach them all a lesson. And if she'd not had other things to do, she would have done it.

Not even bothering to get herself something to eat, she made her way to the highway. It was a frightful thing, the highway. The cars seemed to drive faster all the time. But as she got her way into the moving traffic, not at all bothered by the horns tooting all around her, Caroline counted to one hundred to get herself under control again.

Caroline didn't bother looking at the cars going around her that seemed to have their hands glued to their horns. She knew what the speed limit was, but she didn't care to be killed by driving faster than she could ride a bike. It had been a long time since she'd been able to ride one, but glancing at her speedometer, she knew that fifty was a good speed. If they wanted to follow the rules and drive seventy, then they were all cattle. Follow the herd, she thought. That's all they were good for anyway.

The first thing she was going to have to do was find her a nice place to stay. Caroline didn't care for spending her hard-earned money on such things, but she didn't want to sleep in her car either. It was all right for those that didn't bother with trying to better themselves, but she had. Caroline was educated. She was someone they should aspire to be.

Rachel had to be taken care of first and foremost. Killing her wasn't out of the question, but Caroline would try to resolve this calmly, without slinging bad or dirty names at each other, or any of the other low brow things that she knew Rachel did. She'd heard the way that Rachel spoke to her father, and there wasn't any way that she was going to put up with that bologna.

Then there was the boy. David would be coming to her home if it was the last thing she did. He would be trained to be just like his father — a good man, but David would know the meaning of a dollar. He'd know how to save every penny.

Caroline had been robbed four times in her lifetime. All of them had been by Alan, but since he'd not been able to see his butt for the forest, she'd not called the police on him. It was

51

no less than he deserved, but she knew that he'd come back to her, and then things would be fine again.

The tin that she put her emergency money in was in the same place it had been for decades—sitting on her vanity, alongside her one bottle of perfume and her powder duster. That was another thing that she prided herself on. There wasn't a bit of clutter anywhere in her home. If she did not need it, couldn't eat it, then it was trashed.

Caroline didn't recycle either. "Who would want a bunch of things I tossed away, sitting ready to be put in a special bin? Not anyone with any sense. The trash people only want you to do that so that you'll draw all the rats and vermin from their homes to your own. No, not going to do it."

Smiling, feeling better already, Caroline drove until she saw the signs for her exit. While she hated the interstate, it certainly made it faster to get someplace. It had taken her the better part of an hour to write the instructions down after finding the map that she'd picked up for free years ago.

The town that she had to drive through was nice. Trees were blooming, and flowers decorated the outside each one of the little shops. Caroline even enjoyed the lights in the trees that seemed so festive. Pulling into the little parking lot that was next to the bed and breakfast, she got out of her car with her one case and went inside. They had better have her a room, was all she could think about.

"Hello. Can I help you?" She told the elderly woman behind the counter that she wanted a room. "We can do that. How many nights are you staying with us?"

It was on the tip of her tongue to tell her that she was staying by herself, but decided to let it go. There was going to be a nice bed in this deal if she held onto her temper a little while longer.

Caroline told her just two nights. As she was paying up, she asked about her niece, Rachel Spencer. Rachel wasn't stupid, but she would have made some sort of lasting impression on anyone that she met. The woman frowned as she thought of her question.

"Rachel? I'm not sure. If you mean Ray Stanton, yes. I suppose that could be short for Rachel. Could that be her?" Caroline told her that it was a stupid name, and she didn't use vulgar nicknames. "I'm sorry. But that's all I know this young woman by. Perhaps that's not who you're demanding if I know."

The tone nearly had her smacking the woman, but just as she was setting down her case to do so, one of the biggest, fattest policemen she'd ever seen came waddling in. Caroline gave him the once over and dismissed him. Even at her age, she was in better shape than he was.

"This woman is looking for someone called Rachel Spencer." The man laughed and said that was her. Her brother called her Ray-Ray sometimes. "Oh yes. I forgot about David. However, he's not a Spencer any longer either. He's a Stanton as well. Ray's name isn't Spencer anymore. She's married that nice young Levi Stanton. He's an artist."

"Why in God's name is she doing something so stupid as getting married? And to an artist? Everyone knows that is a nice term for a lazy fart that will be working her to the bone and taking all her money. Next you're going to be telling me that she's in the delicate way." The woman looked at the officer, than back at her. "No, I won't have it. I want to have them both arrested. There will be no marrying while I'm alive. Especially not to an artist. I want to press charges against this bum. I want him put in jail. That is, if you can waddle your butt out to where they're flopping, no doubt, and pick him up."

"Now see here—you can't talk to me that way. I'm an officer of the law." She asked him how many officers he was. He looked like he'd eaten the entire force. "Donna, I want you to call Levi and Ray and tell them that there is a person here, a thing, that is demanding I arrest them. Tell them that I have her butt down at the jail."

Before she could understand he was talking about her, Caroline was cuffed up and being dragged—dragged—to the police car. Of all things. And she'd been wrong about his weight deterring him and making him slow. He had her in the back of the cruiser before she could kick him more than a few times.

Someone was going to pay for this, and Rachel was going to be the one. All this trouble she was causing her was being calculated in her mind, and Caroline never forgot a cruel thing done to her. Yes, Rachel and her deadbeat husband, or whatever he was, they were going to pay dearly.

It took her only thirty minutes to pay her bail and get out. Making her way to where she needed to be to take care of things on her own, Caroline mentally ticked off a list of things that she would need to get taken care of. The nerve of these people, thinking that she was a bad person in all this. She only wanted things to go her way, and by golly, they would too. Or heads would roll.

Chapter 5

"I tell you, Ray, it was the best time I've had in a long time. And I did what you asked — I did save you the seeds. She just tossed them away like they was nothing. Your grandma, she'd been saving them for years, she told me. Some of them seeds are older than you are." Ray laughed with Russel, as he had insisted that she call him. "I've wrapped up the other things that she didn't find worth her time too. When she left here, she didn't pick up the envelope that was for her. I don't know what it says, but if you see her, which I think you will soon, then you can give it to her. Is that all right?"

"Yes, of course. I'm to understand that there are a couple of warrants out for her arrest too." He said that she'd destroyed nearly a whole day of donuts by making a scene. "That would be her. Nothing is ever right unless she can toss a few things around. Tell the manager to send me the bill for all the damage. I'll gladly pay for them."

"I'll do that, honey. I have to say, you're so much like your grandma that it boggles my mind that this woman is your aunt." Ray looked over at the information that had been given to her by Dane not an hour ago. "I dearly loved your grandma. She helped me go to law school, and then when I was out, she found me a nice building and clients. I was very jealous that she'd had her own attorney for some time by then. She certainly was someone to look up to."

"Mr. Butler, I'm in need of a business attorney, and my grandma told me that you'd make a good one for me. I've been using someone from the courthouse when necessary, and online. But I'm thinking of expanding my place of business and moving everything here." He asked her if she was going to be building at the new business district. "I am. My husband and his family are here, and I find that I want to be close as well. Can you look into that for me? I'll need a contractor that I can trust, as well as a crew that will do things my way."

"I can do that. In fact, I'm betting that if you want to use pack for that, you'll save a great deal of money, and the pack master will be highly grateful as well." She said that she knew Nate. "Good. I would guess that you would, now that I think on it. I'll get with you later in the week. After your dealings with your aunt are finished."

"All right then."

As Ray hung up the phone, she sat back down at the big desk that had been in storage. Levi had had the family go and gather up all that she she'd gotten from her grandma's place. While they'd been there, she'd gone to her offices to talk to her staff, and also to tell them what her plan was. It was something that she'd been telling them about for a while, but she was still a little startled by their reactions.

"I'm expanding the line to include not just indoor furniture, but I'm going to also try my hand at some outdoors things. Not just patio things, but also things for camping and trips to amusement parks. While I was laid up, I worked out a couple of the designs in my head. I'm sure that you'll like them." They applauded. "But, because of the expansion, I've also decided to move the plant and production to Ohio."

"Great. It's about time."

Ray had looked at Hailey, who had come with her, and frowned when Jack, one of her employees, spoke. The others, all of them, chimed in as well. Everyone was thrilled to be able to be a part of the growth of her company. There were other comments as well.

"I think living in Ohio will be cheaper for me and my kids. Safer too."

"There has got to be less traffic.

"I'll be able to ride my bike without being injured, I hope."

It went on and on about the things that they could do. But her favorite one was that each of them thought they could afford their first home living in Ohio. Ray was thrilled to death that she didn't have to hire a whole new crew.

Hailey was sitting across from her, and Dane was talking on her cell phone to her boss. While she had heard of her boss, Ray, like most of the country, thought him to be a mobster. But it turned out he was working for the government, and trying to make himself an honest living. And in doing so, he had made a great many enemies. That was what Dane did for him — kept him safe.

"How sure is she about this information? Not that I don't believe her, but this is...this is mind blowing." Hailey told Ray that if Dane had found it and shared it, then it was true. She looked at Ray's grandma's Bible. And then there were the markings on Julian's table that he'd gotten from Alma.

"The dates that are on the table are also in the book. Your grandma had very lovely handwriting too, by the way." Ray just nodded at Dane when she joined them again. "There was also an embroidered tapestry that was found in your storage unit. That didn't mention much, but it gave me the first clue."

Allie came just as they were sitting down to lunch, and brought Lucy with her. Tess had been called in for surgery or she'd have been with them as well. Full force four was what Denny had started calling them, and Ray loved it.

Levi was in the studio, doing some outlines and putting together canvas's with Ken. Things out there were a mess, but then she had found out that it was actually a lot neater than normal. She might have to hire someone like Ken to clean up after her before she opened the new plant.

"We've been working with the town in getting a street fair going. We have people on it, but I was wondering what I can count on the three of you to show off?" Dane asked if it had to be something to sell. "No, I don't think that would be necessary. Why? What did you have in mind? Nothing dangerous, I hope."

"No. I used to give these displays about guns and ammo. Kids and adults both like it. They try and match up which ammo type can be fired out of which weapon. All the weapons have been disabled, the firing pins have been removed, but they still enjoy handling them and holding them for the weight. It's as big a hit as gun shows." Allie thought it was a great idea. "Thanks. People are usually timid about it at first, but they get over that when I hand a gun to a kid. Safety first, however. They wear goggles and a vest when they touch one of my weapons."

"On that theme, I could give a few lessons on self-defense.

You know, something along the lines of kicking the shit out of someone when they come up behind you. I did that too, went to gun shows and showed them what you could do if they took your gun, or you stupidly forgot it at home." Lucy looked at Allie. "I'm sure that she can figure out something that has nothing to do with violence, Lucy. Don't look so terrified."

They were laughing when Ray was told she had a phone call. Getting up, she made her way to the office to take the call. She had several things going on right now, and one of them was the interviews for a company to come in and pack her things up to bring here. She had been given use of an old building downtown in the meantime.

Answering the call with a simple "Hello," Ray was startled to hear from her aunt.

"Where are you, Rachel? I have been all over this town asking questions, and all I get is, 'she's such a nice girl.'" Caroline had used a whiney voice that Ray was sure no one in town had used. "I demand that you tell me where you are this moment, young lady. I have been informed about the will, and I have come for David. And my share of the money."

"David is not going anywhere. Especially not with you. And I don't have any idea why you traveled here. I have nothing to give you. Grandma's will was very clear on who got what. And since Alan didn't get anything other than his bills paid off, there is nothing there either." Caroline made a point to make sure that she heard her counting to ten. "You do that well. Is that supposed to mean something to me? That you're all badass? I'm not a child anymore, Caroline. And you'll figure that out soon enough."

"You will have respect for me, Rachel, or so help me,

you'll learn it some other way. And Alan is Father, not Alan, to you. As for his things from Mother, we'll just have to see about that, won't we?" Caroline huffed. "Where is David? As I stated before, you're to bring him to me. Alan made it very clear that I was to raise him into a better man."

"Better man than him? Your brother? I have a husband and a new family that is doing that for him now. And believe it not, despite who his father was, David is a good student, and a better son for me than he might be under your care." Caroline asked her what she meant about him being her son. "Didn't you hear? I adopted him as mine when the courts said that Alan was unfit to raise him—something about abusing him all the time. But then, you'd know all about that, wouldn't you? But I adopted him then. And when I married, my husband did the same."

"I never said that you could do that. You will have that voided right this minute, or so help me, Rachel, you'll rue the day in disobeying me." Ray looked at her friends, who had joined her in the office, and she gathered strength from them. "I swear to Christ, I should have smothered you too."

"What did you just say to me?" Caroline didn't answer her. "Did you just tell me that you should have smothered me too? Who are you talking about? My mother? You killed my mother?"

"You'd be better off thinking about what I'm going to do to you when I get there. Now, tell me where you are. I'm sick of getting the runaround in this town." Rachel hung up the phone. It was that or make a fool of herself by crying to Caroline. When the phone rang again, she simply walked away from it. Dane and the rest of them followed her out to the deck.

"She did, you know." Allie spoke softly, but Ray had no trouble hearing her. "It was in the paperwork that we unearthed for you. Caroline was in the room when your mother passed away. It was thought that was what had happened, but before they could have her body examined by a physician, Alan shipped her body off to be cremated."

"Caroline is coming for David and whatever was left from my grandma to me." She looked at the rest of them. "I want her out of my life, and I think short of killing her, I'm not going to be able to do anything about her. I'm nothing like she is. Or Alan."

"No, you are not, dearie." Lucy got up and hugged her after sitting on the swing with her. "I'm very proud of you for making something of your life. And taking care that your grandmother didn't have to go without. Nor that young man of yours. I have to tell you, he's a great deal of fun in the kitchen. We made strawberry jam and jelly just yesterday."

Ray smiled. David could speak of nothing else but the Stantons and how they treated him. And not once, he'd told her, had any of them hit him—which, she supposed, was the most important thing to both of them. And Levi and he were getting along so well, people thought that he was a relative of his, and talked about how much David resembled him.

"She's here. At the bed and breakfast. I do hope that she doesn't cause that nice woman any trouble." Dane said that she had people in place that knew not to take her shit. "Good. And if they have to take care of her, then I do hope that you have a nice plot for her far away."

"Oh, you don't have to worry about that, Ray. I have ways of making it so that no one will ever find her, ever. Not even the smallest drop of blood." Ray thought it was the smile that churned up her belly, that and the honest way Dane had said it. Like there was never any doubt about her methods. "First thing we need to do is, find out if you have any powers that might have gotten passed on to you. You'll need to learn to control them a little."

~*~

Levi wasn't sure if he was relieved or disappointed that Ray had no powers whatsoever. She could read minds like Hailey, but that was the extent of her abilities from Dane. He hugged her when she looked at him so sadly, then closed his eyes and held her even tighter.

"Colton told me about a few times he'd startled Hailey and she cut him. It wasn't bad, but it was scary. At least we don't have to worry about that." She looked up at him. "And, you might not believe this, but I think you're perfect just the way you are. My little Ray of sunshine."

"You're a sap." He laughed with her. "I wanted to be able to defend us against my...against Caroline. And not having all those super powers, even just one of them, I can't save you like you did me."

"I'm a cougar." She grinned at him. "And, as Dad has pointed out, you could be too. But we have to wait until this thing is over, especially now that we know she's in town. Also, I've been notified by a couple of contractors. The pack too. Nate said that with both the packs he has now, there are about two hundred that are out of work. And a great many of them have worked on job sites before."

"I was also talking to Mr. Butler. He's going to be my business attorney. I had asked Christian, but he said that he doesn't have a great deal of experience in my sort of business, and I might be better off finding someone that can dedicate all their time to just mine." Levi said that he worked for the family. "Yes, that's what he told me. And for Brayden. I guess he makes sure there are no nasty loopholes in his contracts. Does he find that a lot?"

"You'd be surprised." He nibbled on her neck as he spoke, knowing that they were alone in the house. "Do you have a great deal going on today, Mrs. Stanton? I know for a fact that David is staying out at the pack to make sure that he's safe. How about you and I have some fun?"

"Fun? No, I don't think so." He could have cried. "But, I'd love to make love with you. All over the house, one room at a time. You don't want—"

Her laughter was so wonderful to hear when he picked her up and carried her to their room. She was breathing in his scent at his throat even as he shut the door behind them when they got upstairs.

She'd been ordering things from her plant to come to the house. He put her down on the floor and went to the bed. It was magnificent—and huge. He asked her where she'd found a mattress to fit it.

"We have to order them from another company that deals in specially made mattresses. I was surprised how many people get the bed even though they know that the mattress isn't standard. But it works out well for us both. Also, we make the sheets for it in house, so that helps. I'm hoping to be able to increase the manufacturing of those when we move here." He touched the large quilt that was on the bed. "That was made by my grandma. She loved making them so that they'd be big enough to share with someone. It was what inspired me to make a bed that this would fit. And I think it looks great with this type of furniture."

"It's beautiful. And the canopy? You make those as well?" She said that it was tatting work that had been done a very long time ago by her grandmother's mother. "This is so lovely, Ray. And I love that it has drawers under it for extra storage."

"All the pieces that I make have more than one use. This bed, for instance, can be made into a crib and grows with the child. It's just a matter of changing out the extra pieces that are hidden between the drawers under the bed." Instead of looking, he sat down on the bed and told her to come to him. "I've thought of nothing else but having you inside of me. Having you take me apart with sex. Not only that, but touching me. I have to admit, sex before was just a way to relive some tension. It was neither fulfilling nor fun. But I have a feeling with you, it's going to rock my world."

"You going to rock my world, Ray? I hope so. Because I can't take any more cold showers." She giggled, and he smiled at her. "Take off your clothing. I want to see all of you. We've been married for three days, and I've yet to see any part of you but your face and hands."

She unbuttoned the buttons on the shirt that she'd borrowed from him. Things were still coming in, mostly her clothing and things she had in storage, but she said she needed more. He loved seeing her in his things, and thought they could wait forever if he could see her wearing his things all the time. When the shirt came off, he realized that she was braless, and he swallowed twice before he remembered that he had to breathe too.

"I rarely go without a bra, but I thought that I could entice you if I went without one for a few hours. They hurt when I do that. Can you make them all better for me?" He nodded, unsure if he could talk and breathe at the same time. Pulling her to him when she was close enough, he suckled at one, then the other before she backed from him. "I'm still dressed. But then, so are you. I'm assuming that you aren't as needy as you thought? Should I purchase myself some toys when you're like this?"

"You are playing with fire, love. Christ, do I want you." He stood up and jerked his shirt open. Buttons went everywhere, and he was glad that it made her moan. His pants were in tatters on the floor next to the shirt she'd had on. "I want to paint you. In the nude. I want to cover your entire body with different colors, and have you roll on a canvas for me. I think that you'd make a wonderful model."

"That sounds like fun." He pulled her to him again. "Levi, I have never wanted a man like I do you. And I think if you linger too long in just looking at me or touching me, I'll come with that alone."

Picking her up, he took her to the wall. He had so wanted to use the bed, but she needed him, and who was he to turn down the needs of his mate? But instead of slamming into her, he held her up, entering her as slowly as his body would allow him to. Her face, her reactions, were more than he could have hoped for.

He made love to her like that for several minutes. She came for him three times, and still wanted more. Pressing his body to hers so that they were touching everywhere, she wrapped her legs around him, and Levi took her mouth as he took her body. Hard. Fast. And hotly.

"I'm coming." Ray screamed this time, her body nearly unseating him as he fucked her harder. Taking her to the bed, he didn't let her go but continued to fuck her like his life depended on it. He needed her to come with him, to taste him as he did so. Touching her body, her breasts, face, and hands, Levi told her as only an artist could what he thought of her skin, her beauty, and the way her muscles bunched and held him as he did.

"Do you have any idea how long I've waited for you? For my mate to come to me, to make me feel like I'm the luckiest man alive?" Ray screamed again and again that she loved him. "Bite me, Ray. I need to know that you're mine, that you taste of me, that I taste of you too."

When her teeth sank into his shoulder, he cried out—not in pain, but in complete pleasure. Levi felt like his knees no longer had the muscles needed to hold him up. Even his fingers tingled with the feeling she gave him by biting him. But before he could say anything, if there was anything for him to say, he felt his own release race over him and Levi cried out.

The roar of his cougar made him weak with the release. He knew for a fact that he came with him, that his cat had as much if not more sexual pleasure than he had. As they both lay there, their mate out cold, Levi had to think about slowing his heart, making his breathing less erratic. It was all he could do to roll over so that he wasn't crushing her, and then covering them both with the quilt on the bed.

When woke, he could hear Ray. Whoever she was talking to, the conversation wasn't going well. Getting up, pulling on his boxers as he went, he found her in the bathroom on the floor. She looked up at him, and he could tell that she'd been crying. Holding her hand, he waited for her to tell him who it was.

"I'm glad that you have an attorney, Caroline. But that

won't do you spit, since I have one too. And just so you know, you'll never get to David. He is someplace even you might be afraid to enter into." Caroline asked her again where he was and when Ray was bringing him to her. "Never. And do not call me again. I will have my attorney call yours, and we'll meet someplace where there won't be any ambushes on your end."

"Ambush? You make it sound as if I'm some sort of monster." Ray said that she was. "Young lady, you will stop this nonsense right this moment and stop trying to show off by being this hard person that we both know you're not. Why, at the first sign of me coming at you with a switch, you would crumble like a stack of cards."

"It's a house of cards, you moronic fuck, and you'll regret the day that you tangled with me, you old bitch. Because now that I'm older, you'll find that I'm a great deal stronger where you're concerned." She cut off the call as her aunt was still speaking. "She called here and I didn't recognize the number. I should have gotten the ones from the pack. I thought it might be them."

"I'm going to get in touch with Nate now and tell him to be on the lookout for Caroline. Like you said, I don't think she'll be able to find David, but I don't want to take any chances that Caroline isn't as stupid as she looks." He asked her if she was all right. "If you'd like, I thought that the two of us could go into Columbus and have a nice dinner to celebrate our wedding. As well as the fact that I got paid today."

"Yay. I'm sure that you are going to spend it wisely." He laughed. "I would love to go to dinner with you. Are you sure that David will be all right? If she gets him, I'll kill her. Because I know what sort of person she is. And the way she's been acting lately is nothing compared to what I know she can turn into when she gets riled up."

"Well, we'll just have to rile her up. And Dane told me some of the things that had been done by her. I'm sure there are plenty more that have never been reported. She is not someone I'd want to tangle with even if she was having a good day." Ray told him that she was worse than she'd heard Vonda had been. "Holy Christ, don't tell that to Brayden. I think he still has nightmares about her. And that's not a joke. That woman was insane and violent."

He told her a couple of the things that Vonda had done while she'd been staying at Mom's house. The roses were all replanted now, and Mom had gotten herself some new blooms too. Levi also told her how Vonda had stabbed Brayden in the hand when he'd been trying to tell her that he wasn't human, that none of them were.

"She sounds like a peach. What do you think would have happened if Dane or any of the others would have had to go toe to toe with her?" He told her that she'd be dead. "Yes, Dane scares the fuck out of me. And the other three do too. But it's your mom that has the biggest effect on me. She can smile, using her lovely happy voice, and tear you apart before you knew what was happening. Your mom is what I call a calm scary. And if she were to lose her temper with a person, I'd run and hide. There wouldn't be any second chances with her."

Levi didn't know where she might have gotten her information, but he believed that Ray might be right. He'd seen his mom peel the skin off of a person when she was angry, and never raise her voice. His dad, when he heard her talking like that, did indeed step back and out of her way,

Levi just realized. Laughing, he told Nate what was going on as they were pulling out of the driveway. Tonight was going to be about the two of them.

Chapter 6

Caroline was so mad that she could feel her head pounding with it. Rachel was going to have to learn her place if she wanted to have any more dealings with her. Not that she thought they were going to have anything to do with one another after Caroline had David, but she never knew. The stupid girl might come around to her way of thinking once she had David where she wanted him.

She'd been working on a list of things that David was going to have to be untrained on and trained about. He would learn manners, first of all. And he'd know how to come to the table dressed. Not like these fools that were sitting around her in the restaurant.

Caroline had on her best. Her heels were polished and her collar ironed stiff. The hat was old, but it had held up nicely. There was no skimping on clothing at her home. And once you got it, you wore it until it no longer was serviceable. And even after that, she'd find some use for it.

Like her living room cushions. When a dress was too bad to

wear out even in the back yard, she would cut it down herself and recover her cushions. That was why she was careful of the colors of clothing that she purchased. So that no matter what color the cushions were, it went along nicely with the living room. And her underthings, the unmentionables, were also reused. She'd keep those around to make small hot pot holders, as well as cleaning rags. Everything had a purpose, and then a repurpose.

The woman that had taken her order came to ask her if she'd like a refill on her tea. It was very good, but Caroline would never say it to her face. She took pride in only giving out compliments when she deemed them commendable. There were few that deserved any as far as she could tell with this world.

After having a second little ceramic pot of tea brought to her, she looked over the other patrons. Most of them looked as if they'd just rolled out of bed and come here. A couple of them had been working on motors. They smelled of not just grease, but gasoline as well. Nasty people. Their hands were even dirtier than the dirt outside. When Mabel came back with her salad, just the way she'd ordered it, Caroline spoke to her.

"Do you know any Stantons?" She said that she knew all of them. "All of them? Just how many of them are there?"

"Well, there is Dr. and Mrs. Stanton. They come by on Thursday nights for dinner. Then there are their six sons. Five of them are married now, and two of them are going to have a baby. So I guess there might be a lot more than that now." She grinned at her. "I went to school with Jules. He's about the nicest person you could meet. They all are."

"I only asked you if you knew them, and how many. I

72

did not ask you for your life history. What do I care if they're married or not? Believe it or not, I don't care. Now, if you think you can answer me without spewing out information that I didn't ask for, I want you to tell me where they live. All of them."

"Oh, well, I'm afraid that you're shit out of luck there. If a stranger doesn't know where they live, then they're just going to have to figure that out on their own." Mabel leaned down to her eye level and smiled. "You speak to me that way again, and I swear to you, you'll need a hose down your throat to get food to your nasty belly."

Caroline could not believe how that woman had spoken to her. Looking around for someone to help her with the manager's name, she asked the people next to her. She couldn't believe that the woman that had been so harsh with her was the owner. Caroline was going to make it so she lost her license when she got home, by calling the health department on her.

Just as she was ready to go back to her room, her food was set in front of her. Caroline might have been pissy about it, but as far as she could see, it was perfection. Even the steam rolling off the cornbread looked appetizing. Picking up one of them, she opened the crock that was on the table, thinking that it was butter, and was surprised and pleased that it held both honey and butter. Caroline had to put her knife down for a moment—she was trembling with anticipation.

Not only was it as good as it looked, but she thought perhaps the next time she came in, she'd just get several hunks, what Mabel called them, of the cornbread and eat that. But then she looked at her platter of food. There was even an extra plate for her to put as much as she wanted on it.

The fried chicken was browned to a beautiful shade of

mocha. The green beans had tiny bits of onions in them, as well as ham. Caroline didn't care for bacon in her green beans, and was so happy to see that they'd done them correctly. There were mashed potatoes, white gravy, and slaw. Not the kind she normally ate, but what was called sour slaw. It was by far the best tasting dinner she'd ever enjoyed.

Caroline was pleasantly full when a group of loud people came into the little place. They were huge, all of the men, and when the elderly woman told them to behave, they straightened up right then. She was thinking that she would like this woman when she leaned over and kissed the elderly man with her.

It was disgusting, this show of affection. And Caroline didn't have any trouble standing up to the people. Size did not matter when you were on the side of being right about things. And manners were something that she knew all about.

"What is wrong with you two? Can't you see that there are people here eating? Don't do that again, or so help me, I'll teach you how to act in public myself." The woman flushed brightly, and the man looked confused. The other men with her—more than likely she was showing off to them—looked at Caroline like she was something out of a horror picture. "Public shows of affection are bad manners. You should know better than to act like a floozy when you're around other people."

"I'm sorry, who are you talking to?" The bigger of the younger men looked at the couple and then back at her. "You cannot be talking about my parents. Because if you are, I'll wipe the fucking floor up with your scrawny ass."

"Brayden, that's all right." He started to fuss with the woman, but she looked at Caroline. "Some people don't like when others have it better than them. Just let her go. She's probably a dried up old turnip anyway."

"I beg your pardon?" Caroline watched the woman stiffen her back and then pointed at her. "You are very rude calling me names. I will not have it. You'll tell me that you're sorry right now, or I shall have to hurt you."

"Hurt me?" The woman laughed and looked around the room. "Lady, I don't know what your deal is or who might have pooped in your dinner, but you'd better back on up out of my grill, or I'll take you to task."

The woman told her to sit down, but Caroline was not ready. She had a lesson to teach here, and she wasn't going to be denied her apology. While she was stomping her way to the table, another person came in the door just as the other five were being seated. Dismissing her as not being any sort of trouble, Caroline started for the table where the older woman was.

"You will not just turn your back on me. Did you hear me? I said that you owe me an apology. Now, you get up and give it to me. I'm not one to be trifled with. You'll soon learn that." The woman, the newcomer, asked if there was a problem. "No. If I thought there was, I certainly wouldn't call on anyone like you. Get your face out of mine before I rearrange it for you."

The room as a whole moved back from them. Chairs scraped along the floor, and one even fell backwards. Caroline wondered what was going on when the people at the counter, who were just drinking their coffee, picked up their cups and moved back as well. The only people that didn't move were the five sitting at the table and the woman. Caroline turned to her when she thought she could slap her and finish with the older woman.

"You have got to be Caroline Spencer." She didn't know what to say to that, so raised her chin up and looked down her nose at her. "Yessiree. Caroline Spencer just threatened little old me. Whatever should I do?"

The woman put her hand over her heart as if to calm it. Good, Caroline thought, this was what she'd been trying to do with the others—instill the fear of her into them. But there was a tone to her voice that grated on Caroline's nerves. Drawing back to hit the younger one in the face, she stopped when the girl smiled at her. There was something very scary about her smile that had Caroline pausing just for a moment.

"You had better think twice about what is going on in your head, Caroline. In case you didn't realize that you've bitten off more than you can chew, I'm Dane Stanton. That might not mean all that much to you right now, but it will if you hit me. So, why don't you turn your little ass around and get the fuck out of here while you can still walk upright? Otherwise I'm going to break every fucking bone in your body." Caroline asked her who she was supposed to be. The people at the table laughed. "They're my family. And I will protect what is mine, by killing you or making you hurt every time you take a breath. Because if you touch any of them, or me, there won't be any place you can go that children and adults alike will not cringe from what I've done to you."

"She kissed him." Dane looked at the table of people, then back at her. "I do not care for public shows of affection, and I will not have it while I'm eating. That is by far the most disgusting thing I've ever witnessed."

"Kissing?" Caroline crossed her arms over her breast and nodded. "You have got to be joking. You're disgusted by someone kissing? What the fuck, lady? They're married, and have been for a good long time. Kissing?"

When the woman went to the table and jerked the man sitting there up, she kissed him. If that wasn't gross enough, she was picked up by her bottom and actually wrapped her legs around the man's body. Fire burned though her. Caroline could not see straight, she was so angry. And when she jerked the woman back from the man, a gun touched her forehead.

"Dane, let her go." She pouted. Dane's lower lip was sticking out so far that Caroline was sure that she would trip over it if she were to take a step. "While I thank you for detaining her, I'd like to talk to her a moment before you finish your actions."

"But she messed with me." There was a tone that sounded whiney and sad. "Can't I—I don't know—can't I just mess around with her a bit more? I swear to you, no one would believe that she didn't deserve it."

Laughter rang out throughout the diner, and she wanted to look to see who had done it. But the big man standing next to Dane was smiling too. He should know better.

"You think this is funny? This woman just kissed you and nearly had you on the floor for unspeakable acts, and you think it's funny?" He said that it had been fun. The elderly lady told the man to behave. "I'm afraid it's much too late for you to learn any lessons, sir. What you will need to have done to you is being strapped to a tree and having it beat into you."

"You mean as you did me?" She looked at the woman. It took her a second to realize who it was. "Yes, it's me. Ray. And if Dane would be so kind as to allow you to have a seat, you and I can talk before you leave town. Also, I have a letter for you from Grandma. I took the liberty of reading it. She said to tell you that you're a waste of air. And that she should have told you that while she was alive. There's more of the same. I can show you if you'd like."

"No, I do not want to see it. She wasn't right in her head. And anything she had to say to me was nothing to me. I'm going to tell you right now, Rachel, I'm not leaving here without David. You will not raise him properly, and I won't have you ruining him with your evil ways." Rachel asked her what she was talking about. "Just look at you. You're dressed for the streets. Is that how you make your living, Rachel? You use innocent men and take their money, ruin their homes? I wouldn't put it past you. No, you're a bad influence on David, and I mean to have him trained in the correct way of dealing with people such as these and you. There are ways to beat out what you've misled him about, and I'm going to do it."

She was let go, but didn't move back. She was still intent on getting these people to tell her that they were sorry for ruining the dinner of herself and everyone in the diner. With her arms still crossed over her breasts, Caroline tapped her foot, a sure sign that she was upset and wanted these people to know it. Rachel had been gone too long to remember her ways of dealing with things, or she would have heeded her warning. But when the young chit snapped her fingers and pointed at the chair, Caroline felt the need to do whatever Rachel wanted of her.

"Caroline, sit down."

There was nothing to do but sit. As much as she wanted to stand up, tell Rachel that she couldn't talk to her that way, she was afraid of her. The voice she used, it sounded inhuman. Waiting for her to calm down the others in the place, Caroline thought of what sort of treatment this child was going to receive from her.

It made her equally mad when Rachel offered to pay for dinner for everyone in the diner for the trouble that her aunt had caused, and said that she was very sorry. Caroline should have been the one that was being apologized to, not this group of nobodies.

~*~

"I thought I told you to leave town." Caroline raised her chin but said nothing. "I see. You're going for the 'I'm so much better than you' scenario, are you? Well, it won't work with me anymore. I've had enough shit going on in my life that you're not even a blip on my radar anymore. What do you want? Besides David. Who you are not going to get."

"I have your father's will that states that I am to raise him. You will turn him over to me, or so help me, Rachel, you'll regret it. I'm sick to death of getting the runaround from you. And you will obey me." The elderly woman smiled at her. "Or have you forgotten what it is I do to you when you disobey me? Surely you have a few scars left on your back. Or do you need a refresher course on how much I hate you?"

"No, that won't be necessary. You'll be happy to know that I have absolutely no love for you too." Ray could see that had shocked her. "What? You don't think I have just cause to hate you? Well, let me give you a little refresher course. How about the fact that you held me tied up and gagged as you beat poor David until he bled? He was only six years old. Or the time you tied me to the hood of your car and drove around and around in the field by the house to see if I could hang on. Because, if I remember, you had David in the trunk, and said if I fell off, you'd kill him. No, I have every reason in the world to hate you. And you are not getting my brother."

79

"We'll just see about that."

Ray didn't want to talk to her. Didn't want to be breathing the same air as she was. But when she'd heard from Dane that she was going to have to kill her, Ray thought it best to come down and keep her friend out of jail. Not that, like she said, it wouldn't be justified, but there was all that paperwork to fill out, and then she'd have to take care of the mess she would have made in the diner. Because there was no doubt in her mind that Dane would have made a very big mess with Caroline.

"You killed your father. What do you have to say about that?"

"Nothing. And yes, thanks, I'm still alive after he nearly killed me. And don't tell me that I did a thing to him. I have it on video what he did to me before he was caught. I nearly died that day." She huffed at her. "You'll be surprised to know that he didn't mean shit to me. This might come as a surprise to you as well, but you don't mean shit to me either. Never since you tied me to the tree out back of your home and beat me until I could neither walk nor breathe on my own. Thankfully the neighbors didn't like you, or there is no telling how long I would have hung there, you fucking bitch."

"Watch your language. I did not raise you to curse like a sailor." Ray told her that she'd had very little to do with her upbringing. "Because Mother had to have you with her, for God only knows what reason. She let the two of you, you and David, get away with everything, I'm betting. Watching that nasty television. She should have died a very long time ago. You would have been a lot better of a person had you been with me. Or, as you pointed out, I might have buried you in the back yard. It would have been easier on all of us had you died too. Where are Mother's nice things? Did you sell them off for that outfit you're wearing? It doesn't impress me, Rachel. You're a bad person no matter what you put on your body. I want her things in compensation for having to have her as my mother all these years."

"I don't have anything that belonged to you. If that's your way of asking me politely if I have her jewelry, I do. I'm having it cleaned and appraised. Then it'll be put in the safe with the other things that my husband has given me." She asked her what husband. "The one that I'm married to. Levi Stanton. He loves me, as does his family. It's a nice feeling, being loved. Has anyone ever loved you? I'm doubting it."

"Don't be obtuse, Rachel. I no more believe that you have a husband than I do." She asked her if she ever did. "No. What need would I have for a man in my life?"

"To have children. A person that loves you and someone you can depend on. Didn't you ever want that in your life?" Ray was glad that she was looking at Caroline when she said that. There was just a second of something there, but nothing more. "What? You wouldn't like to have a child bouncing on your knee? Someone to call you Grandma?"

"Disgusting. Especially if they were anything like you were as a child." She asked her why she wanted David then. "There is still hope for him. I'll train him to learn what is right and wrong. The meaning of saving his money. Also, he'll be getting a fine education when he comes to live with me."

"Sounds like a plan. It's really too bad that you won't have anyone to execute it with. You're not going to touch him." Ray stood up, suddenly just tired of dealing with her. "I'm going home. Caroline, please remember this. My family is not ones to fuck with. And you weren't killed today because I came here to save your ass. Next time, I might be too busy to come. Just stay away from my family, and you might just live a bit longer."

Leaving the restaurant, she tried to tell herself that she was stronger than her aunt. That she was in the right. But her actual feelings were that she was defeated. That she couldn't keep up this appearance of being strong much longer. She looked to her right when someone joined her.

"You want my advice." Ray told Dane that she wasn't going to kill her, not just yet. "Spoil sport. No, that wasn't my advice. Good advice, but not what I was going to say. I think the two of us need to go over to the job site and see if we can see a couple of half-naked men and compare them to our husbands."

Ray stopped walking, and it took Dane a few more steps before she stopped and looked at her. Sometimes the things that came out of her mouth bordered on insanity. But it did make Ray smile when Dane winked at her. She asked her what she really wanted.

"I do need you at the job site. There is some question about the bathrooms that you want to put in. I think it's a great idea to have four sets of bathrooms on each floor. But they want to make sure that it's correct." Ray told her that it was wrong. "Ah, really? And I so wanted to be right."

"There should be eight. I have a lot of women working for me on the upper floors, and the lower levels need to be something more than a long hall of stalls. They're not safe, for one thing. Anyone could be lurking around there, and I do hate to have to go into one of those things when I'm out, only to find out that there is a long line inside." Dane said that wasn't enough bathrooms. "I know that, so that's why I've made sure that there are those long hall-like johnny systems at each end of the building. But I really think that they're unsafe."

"They are. And you're right about people lurking around. I've dealt with people in bathrooms a great deal." Ray didn't ask, and Dane didn't seem inclined to tell her what she meant. "Okay, I'll drive."

"Oh no you won't. I've heard about the way you drive. Like you have a death wish. And those with you had better have their next of kin on standby. I'll drive." Dane stomped her foot. "Yes, that's very mature. But I'm still driving."

They got in the truck and were headed over when Dane spoke again. "I'd really like to find the person that tells people that. I'd make an example of them." She told her it was Brayden. "Oh. Well, I guess that's all right then. But wait until I have my pilot's license. I'm going to have a great deal of fun with that."

Lord help us, was all Ray could think about as Dane laughed. They pulled into the site just as the ambulance was coming in. Before she could stop and put the truck in park, Dane was out and running to where they were headed. Ray reached out to Levi.

I'm fine, I promise. She asked him if he was the one the ambulance was for. *Yes. I cut myself pretty badly, and since most of the people here don't know me, I'm waiting to get to a quiet place to heal. How did you know?*

"Because I'm here too." He grinned at her when she stood over him. "How on earth did you do this? Not paying attention?"

"No. Well, yes. I was talking to the foreman and leaned onto that piece of equipment. Before I could figure out it was plugged in and on, I had already cut myself." She peeled away the blood soaked towel. "It looks worse than it really is."

"Does it, Levi? Because it looks to me like you sliced through your palm all the way to the bone." He nodded, then laid his head back on the floor where someone had put him. "That is going to be painful no matter how you take care of it."

"I know. Wyatt is coming to sew it up for me." She put the rag back and held his injured hand in hers. "I just wanted to talk to the man about having us a nice place we can go where no one could find us. It seemed like a good idea."

"Yes, because all you ever think about is sex." He laughed, and a couple of the men around them snickered. Glaring at Levi, she told him to behave.

"Me? You're the one that let the cat out of the bag." She could see Wyatt coming into the building. He seemed to be on the phone, as he was having a very loud conversation with someone. "I don't know who he's talking to, but someone has pissed him off. Wyatt isn't one to use a loud voice unless he's really pissed off."

She didn't know who it was, nor did she feel comfortable with him enough to ask. Wyatt, unlike the rest of the men in the family, was quiet. Reserved. And he didn't talk much even in a conversation. But something that she did know about him, that she didn't think the others knew, was that Wyatt wanted a change in his life.

"All right, moron, let me see what you've done to yourself. Just so you know, Levi, I'm going to bill you for this. I was having a nice lunch with this amazingly built...smart woman when you called. She is not happy with me that I had to leave to take care of you." Ray moved out of the way and waited while Wyatt looked at the wound. "If this is a joke, Levi, I do not think it's the least bit funny. I have shit that I'm trying to get organized."

"What? Why would you find me being hurt a joke?" They both looked at the wound and then at her. "Ray? What did you do?"

"Nothing. I was right here with you." They showed her his hand, and then pulled the rag all the way off when there was nothing there. Not even a scar. "I don't know. I didn't—"

Falling back, her last thought was, I guess I got something from Dane after all.

Chapter 7

Levi put the phone back in the cradle. He wasn't sure what to do about everything that was going on right now with his artwork. Just yesterday he'd invited his mom and dad to come into his other world, as Ray called it. Levi had watched as they walked around the room, looking at each piece like they were going to have to tell someone later what it looked like.

"Do you want to talk about it?" Levi smiled at Ray. She'd been out here helping him all morning, and he just wanted to hold her. He asked her about what. "The fact that you were cut to the bone, then you weren't. I won't be mad if you did it on your own."

"I swear to you that I didn't." She nodded, and took out the rest of the trophies and took them to the shelf they were going to be on. "I can test the theory if you want. We can cut me and see if you heal it, or nothing happens. Have you told anyone?"

"No. I mean, the people that were there think it was a

fluke and that you did it. Dane, like you, wants to cut herself up and see what happens." She put some of the taller ones in the back while he handed her the smaller ones. "Tell me again why you hid these away?"

"I don't know, to be honest. I was embarrassed? Ashamed? I think I was afraid that someone would say it was pretentious of me to have them out." She snorted at him. "Don't think I didn't notice that you changed the subject, either."

"I'm afraid." He asked her of what as he helped her off the ladder they'd been using. "That it's real. That I can actually heal someone by just holding their hand or whatever."

Levi waited for her to turn and look at him before he spoke again. "I don't see anything wrong with what you can do. Since you have sworn me to secrecy, I can't ask anyone either."

"How on earth would you even bring that up? Oh, by the way, my wife can heal people, we think. I'm not sure, though, because she's a dumbass and won't let me try it again." He said he'd never call her a dumbass. "Why not? I am one. All I'd have to do is test the theory and that would be it."

"I would never call you a dumbass because I'm afraid of you." She smacked him and he laughed. "I'm going to do it for you now. And then, when you fix me up, we'll be able to share this — No. We'd better not share. I don't know what sort of people would come around and demand that you'd heal them. That would be scary."

"I didn't think of that." Levi told her that he hadn't either, but Dane had. "She has a mind of a criminal, if you ask me. But that's not usually a bad thing. It makes her think outside the box. And from what I'm to understand, that is what keeps her alive."

"I don't doubt that either. She's very cunning, if you ask me." They both laughed. "Are you ready for this? I did my one thing, now it's your turn."

"All right. But is the door locked?"

He said it was, but went to check on it anyway. Levi was going to paint her. And once he was finished with her body, she was going to lay on the canvas that he had laid out for her and roll around. There were so many ideas going through his head at the moment, he almost missed what she said.

"I said, what is the second thing you want me to do? I have one for you."

Yesterday they had decided that they needed to get out of their comfort zone. His was bigger than hers. He had to empty out all his awards and trophies and display them in the front part of his studio. The new building, the one that he'd purchased from his brother, was perfect for that. He was going to be able to use all the natural lighting that he needed, and still have room to store things.

The place that was on their land was going to be used for work that wasn't paint related. Pottery was much too dirty to have around paints, he'd decided long ago. Once he had everything cleared out of the big barn he'd been using, it was going to be a studio for pottery and kiln. Since there was a loading dock on that building, it was going to be perfect to get in supplies in larger quantities as well.

Behind the closed doors, he had her undress and stand up. He tried very hard not to think of this naked vision in front of him. If he gave into his needs, they'd never get this done. Instead of taking her to the floor, he had her pull her hair up in a bun for now, and started with some of his favorite colors.

Before long, he was able to concentrate more on what he was doing, instead of who he was doing it to. And she was a perfect model too, doing what he wanted and moving how he wanted her to. He also needed the silence to work, so she didn't speak unless he asked her a question.

The canvas was nearly ten feet across and twelve feet high. Levi knew what he wanted done on it, but was having trouble getting the colors that he needed to cooperate. It wasn't until she asked if she could take her hair down that he got it. It was another two hours before he thought she was ready.

"Wait." He didn't look at her; the paint all over her body and hair were just what he had envisioned. He was in love with how the colors blended well on her breasts, and looked at her when she didn't speak again. "Join me."

His muse perked up. Not sexually, though he could see them covering the art with their love making. And when she laid on the canvas, waiting for him, he stripped down quickly and joined her. He was glad now that he'd kept the shower in the place. He had a feeling that they were going to need it before this was finished.

When Ray moved around, her body leaving beautiful markings where he wanted, Levi touched her with his hands and smeared it onto the canvas too. Touching her this way, her body slick with the paint, he knew that no one would ever see this canvas. This was going to be theirs.

Levi came up behind her, rubbing his hands over the blues and golds that were there. He curled his hands into her hair and sprayed the paint from his fingers all over the canvas. After a while, he realized that he had just as much paint on his body as she did, and he was having fun.

He couldn't touch her with his mouth — she couldn't him

either—but the way they were touching, smoothing each other's muscles, was enough for him. Making love to her, without having actual intercourse, was just as exciting as any other way he'd made love before.

"I need to come."

He had her lay on her back, her hair making a beautiful kaleidoscope of colors by her head. Levi found a sponge that was clean and rubbed it on her clit. He didn't want her to get an infection from this, but that didn't mean he couldn't have fun too. Stroking his cock, she took the sponge from his free hand and sat up enough to watch him.

The exoticness of what they were doing, the creativity of it, had him coming hard. And when he sprayed his cum all over her body and the canvas, he cried out when she rubbed it on her body then rolled around for him. Ray screamed loudly when she released, and before he could catch his breath, Ray came twice more while the paint was covering the piece.

Levi came twice more in the shower with her. He asked her why they didn't conserve water at home like this, and she laughed.

"Because we'd never get any work done. Wearing each other out, we'd make love, take a nap, and do it again." He said he liked that idea. "Yes, you would. But I have a timeline, and so do you. It's only spring right now, but I have to get my Christmas catalog printed, as well as finish the three things I have going right now."

"You're a party pooper."

They were dried off when he decided that he wanted to see what they'd done. As soon as he entered the studio, Levi knew that this was what he'd been striving for his entire career. He was in love with the work.

"Oh my goodness." Levi said he loved it. "I do too. I just thought it would be a bunch of smeared up paint that looked like you'd had a five year old do it."

"This is what I wanted. I mean, right down to the way your hair made it look like water splashing up over the rocks at the seaside." He walked around it twice, seeing things that he'd not seen the first time around. "This is your breast. My cock is here. No one would know that, of course, but it's beautiful. I had an idea that I wanted to put some sparkle in it—a little faerie dust, so to speak—but I won't now."

Getting the ladder back out, Ray climbed it to have a different view. He was down on his knees, trying to see if he was missing any other element of their bodies. When she asked him to come up, he did so when she came down. From there, he could see it all, and it was even more magnificent than he had thought.

"I'm not saying this because we did this, but honey, this is the best painting I've ever done. We've ever done. I'm not planning on selling it, but—"

"Why not?" He asked her what she meant. "I mean, the thought of someone paying money for us having sex in paint, then hanging it in their living room, is funny to me. They'd have no idea that my breast is there. Or that your cum is there with the blues and golds. I know that it'll dry and no one will ever know, but every time I think of it, I'd smile. Wouldn't you?"

"I'd have to clean that up. I mean, what if they got to close to it or something, and realized what it was." She said that might be smart. "You'd really not care if someone had a painting of us having sex in their home?"

"No. I mean, if it looked like that, then yes, I'd want it

behind locked doors. But no one will know, and just so you know, I'm certainly not going to tell them. Unless your mother wants to know. Then hell yeah, I'm going to tell her." He asked if she was serious about telling his mom. "Sure. I love to see her all flustered, don't you?"

"Absolutely not. I do not want to think about either of us telling my mom what we did here. I have never.... Nope, not going to happen. If she wants this piece, I'll tell her that it's sold, and make sure that even if I have to destroy it, she'll never know." Ray was laughing, and he smiled. She was the best thing that had ever happened to him. "The only thing I have to do is put it up so that it can dry. I figure that it'll take a couple of weeks. And if you really don't mind, I am going to put it in the next show I go to."

"Do it." After she yawned a second time, he asked her if she was all right. "Yes. I was helping David with his homework last night. I'm not so good at the new math. I don't think I can get it through my head."

"No one can, I don't think. But I can talk to Brayden. He's been doing that sort of thing for a while now. He's been tutoring at the school on Wednesday afternoons." Ray told him that would be great. "Now, here we go."

He hadn't meant to cut so deeply, but once he did it, Levi looked at Ray. The stunned look on her face was enough to tell him that he had gone just a little too far. But she came to him, putting her hands over the wound while he watched.

As soon as she took her hands away, he knew that it had healed. What he'd not expected, however, and should have, was the punch to his face from her. He'd tricked her, pure and simple. But now they knew that she could heal someone if they needed. At least, so far she could heal him. Levi wondered how much trouble he'd be in if he cut up one of his brothers when she was around. He'd have to work on that one.

~*~

Ray worked on the mock up for several hours before she looked over at the gadget that Brayden had lent her. It was a three-D printer, and she'd yet to use it. To him, it was like the best invention ever made. To her, it was something else she was going to have to learn how to use. Picking it up, she played with it for several minutes until she got the hang of it. By the time she was outlining the bench she was working on, David had joined her. He asked her what the heck she was doing.

"No idea." She put it aside for now. "Did you have Brayden help you with your math? And was he nice about it too? Dane said he can talk over your head at times, and she has to knock him around a little."

"Nah, it was fine. I got a lot from it. And he didn't use the 'F' word once." She laughed with him. "I was wondering if you and I could go and get a pizza or something. Just us. I have something I need to talk to you about."

"All right. I'm about finished here. Let me tell Levi where we're going and tell him he's on his own."

She was worried about what David might have to tell her. They'd not been spending a lot of time together of late, just the two of them. He'd been at the pack house, hiding out from Caroline during the day, and was fixing his room in the evenings—whatever that meant to a sixteen year old boy.

After they were seated and had their drinks, he asked her where their aunt was. "I've not seen her, if you're going to ask me that. It's a safe bet that she's not leaving until she gets what she wants, huh? I was just wondering if she was going to pop out of the woodwork or something. I don't want her to corner us and hurt someone here." David looked around before continuing. "I'm not going with her."

"As far as I know she's at the B&B—plotting, I would imagine. No, you are not going anywhere with her. You've been taking those self-help classes from Dane, right? I mean, I've noticed that you're not as bruised up as you were when Allie helped you." He said she was teaching him how to use a knife. "Did you cut yourself?

"Not too badly. She said that I will cut myself, and if I'm too big of a pussy about it that I should just let my aunt have me. She's really harsh, isn't she? I mean, I love her very much, but she isn't the motherly type, do you think?"

"Not so much, no. I'll have her get you a knife if you want. One that is suited to what she's teaching you. All right?" He nodded, and she could tell there was something on his mind other than knifes and bruises. "Spill it, big guy. Our pizza is coming soon, and I want to devote my attention to it and not what you're trying hard not to say."

"I like this girl." She nodded, unsure of what she was supposed to do with this. He was nearly seventeen years old. "She's a wolf—one of the pack. I know that I'm not her mate or anything, but she said what we could see a movie or something. Nate said I should be careful and try very hard not to fall in love with her. That would be problematic."

"Oh." He frowned at her and asked if she was mad. "Why on earth would I be mad? I don't know if you realize this or not, but I'm mated with a cougar. And saying not to fall in love is a great deal harder than actually not doing it, don't you think?"

"Yeah, that's what I thought too. The two of us, we

decided it might be better for everyone if we see other people at the same time. You know, spread this man around so to speak. There's only so much loving I can do, you know?" It took her a moment to realize what he was saying, and she laughed with him. "Also, I want to call you Mom and Levi Dad."

"Whoa your horses there. Back up a second. You can't just change subjects like that and expect me to keep up. The wolf-human thing, you don't have to worry about that. You're smart enough to know the right and wrong from that, right?" He nodded. "And you're right, there is just so much that I'll allow you to spread around. Not without using protection. Understand me, young man? Why do you want to call me Mom?"

"There are these kids at school." Ray thought for sure he was going to tell her that they were teasing him or something. "They have all these questions about stuff, and I realized that you guys adopted me. I know it was to protect me, but I love Levi. You? The verdict is still out on you, but I do love Levi."

She tickled him and he laughed. "I don't mind, if that's what you want to do. I think I'd be honored by you calling me Mom. I don't have the first clue how to be one, but I'd love to practice on you." He told her that was another thing that he wanted to talk to her about. "All right. Are we done with the parenting question?"

"Yes. I have to talk to Levi, I know. But I already call Lucy and Denny Grandma and Grandpa. I sure do miss mine, but they love me too." She said that they did, and that she missed Grandma too. "I'm guessing that you guys will have kids someday, right? If you do, what happens to me? I mean, you were going to send me to military school once. Will that be something you do later?"

"We did talk about it, Levi and I. We thought that we'd either hire you out as a brat or simply leave you out with the trash." They both laughed. "David, I would never do that to you. Our kids will be your sisters and brothers. Or, you can tell them that you're their uncle. That would be up to you. You know, when you think about it, that's about as strange as it gets, don't you think?"

"Yes. And I'd tell them that I'm both when they need me. So? No sending me away?" She shook her head. "Thank goodness. I hadn't really thought about it, but Foster, this kid at school, that's what he said his parents were doing to him. They're having a late in life kid, and he's none too happy about it."

"I know this kid, don't I?" David told her who he was. "Ah, yes. He is the one that robbed the grocery store when it was being revamped. Also, I think he's on the hook for driving a car through a cornfield and then leaving it there. I'd send him away too — or beat him. Not really. I don't know how he was raised, but I hope you know that we'd never do anything like that to you. You're a good kid. And you never do stuff like that."

The pizza was set in front of them, and she looked at David when a second one was set down as well. She asked him who they were feeding besides the two of them. His laughter made her feel good. It was like a balm to her heart.

"Levi is coming. Did you know that I can talk to him and all his family? It's kinda cool. But I have to tell you, I called out to him the other day and asked him a question on a test, just seeing if he'd give it to me. He didn't. But he sure was upset with me when he thought that I was cheating. I had to tell him several times that I'd already finished the test. I won't do that again."

Levi joined them several minutes later. David was already starting on the second pizza. She had noticed that her appetite had increased and she was feeling pretty good lately. But she also knew that with all the sex she and Levi were having, she was burning calories quickly. The two of them finished off the second pizza in no time, and they were headed to get ice cream when Levi suddenly stopped walking.

The sidewalk was nearly empty, but she saw her aunt coming toward them before David did. Telling him to not move was all she could do. Protecting him with her body wasn't going to work since he was much taller than her—the same height as Levi. Later, she thought, she was going to think about how much he'd grown.

"There you are. I've come to take you back with me. Come here, David. I will not be thwarted on this any longer. Did you hear what I said? I'm going to take you back with me to make sure you turn out all right. Not like this thing here." None of them moved, and when she reached for his arm, David moved so quickly, even staring at him, she missed it. "What do you think you're doing? Let me go."

The headlock was perfectly done. She would only get away from him if David allowed it. And when he spoke, David's voice sounded low, but firm. Even Ray was a little nervous standing there beside him.

"If you so much as make my parents break a nail over what you do to them from now on, I will hunt you down and make sure that you live to regret it." He let her go and stood there, not moving back one inch. "I'm not now, nor ever, going to live with you or stay with you again. I'm not a child anymore, and the sooner you realize that, the longer I might let you live, Caroline."

"You did this." Caroline looked at Ray and pointed. "You turned him against me with all your lies and secrets. His father said that I could have him. To raise him correctly. And I'll see you dead before I let his last wishes go undone. I'm getting an attorney, Rachel. And I would suggest you do the same."

She started away, limping this time, when she turned back and slapped David in the face. Before he could react, Levi put his hand on David's and told him it wasn't worth it.

"Caroline will get her comeuppance, this I can promise you, David. But if you hit her now, you're going to give her just what she wants. Violence does not need to be met with more violence. Just let's go and get an ice cream, and let the fucking bitch go her way."

David laughed, and when he did, Ray did as well. Caroline was screaming that she was in the right the entire time she walked away.

"The courtroom is where this needs to end with her." Levi said that he agreed with her. "Once this is done and she's out of our lives one way or the other, I'd like to take a vacation and just soak up some sun, lay on some sand somewhere, and have fun. Between the three of us, we should be able to agree on someplace nice, don't you think?"

"You want me to go?" She told David that he was going. "Thanks. Mom, Dad, I just wanted to say how much I love you guys. I decided that I want to be just like you two. I want to be a person to respect, and make a meaningful footprint on this earth. As you can tell, I've been hanging around the pack a great deal."

The trip to the ice cream shop was decided against. They

wanted banana splits, and went to town to get all the things they needed. Ray thought it might have been cheaper, much cheaper, had they gotten them at the shop. But they did have a great deal of fun messing up the kitchen while making them.

Chapter 8

Caroline gathered up her paperwork, and even all the things that had been forged for her long ago. Her mother had been an old poop about things such as being organized. So now that she was gone, things were finally going to go Caroline's way. She'd had to, for many years, tow the line with Mother, but the day that she moved out, she'd become a perfectionist. Unlike her mother, who had so much clutter in her home that she'd never find anything. Much less show it to anyone.

Her attorney was working on setting up a time for the trial. He had wanted to just try talking to the couple, but she had tried that, she told him, and it was a dead end. Mr. Jenkins, who had been working for her for decades, said that her way of talking might not work with these people.

"I have money and they're just working class. There is no reason whatsoever that I shouldn't be raising that boy. And I have to tell you, he's gone downhill since I've seen him last. Why, he assaulted me. Right there on a public street." Mr.

Jenkins asked her what she'd done to him first. "Why, of all the nerve. You don't think I have the right to do as I want? I'm telling you right now, if you don't win this case for me, Jenkins, I will ruin you. He's mine."

"Yes, well, that threat won't work that well on me anymore, Caroline. I'm set to retire after this trial you're insisting on having. Win or lose, you and I are finished as client to attorney. I've been sick of you for years." She asked him what he was talking about. "Well, let's just talk about how much you owe me. Not what you say you do, but what you actually owe me. I do not work on what you think I should be getting as payment, but I have a set amount I charge everyone."

"I will not pay you four hundred dollars an hour for you to talk to me about lawsuits. Minimum wage is all you're going to get from me. Why, I don't even pay the boy who mows my lawn as much as that. You're good, but not four hundred dollars an hour good." He told her that he'd either get it from her or from her estate. "You think so, do you? Well, thanks to you, I have that all tied up, don't I? When I die, I'm going to be the only person in the world that takes it with me. Every penny is going to be lining my casket so that no one can take that from me."

"All someone needs to do is meet you, Caroline, and I'm sure that they can attest that you're insane." She was so shocked by his statement that she didn't get to form a retort before he continued. "I'll have someone from my staff call you when I have a date for the trial. And you should really look up— Wait, that won't work. You won't have anything to do with a computer. Anyway, I do hope you lose. That boy and anyone else that comes in contact with you deserves better. Hell, my dog would deserve better, and he's a mean little shit."

The line went dead and she was still steaming about it. Then an hour later, someone did indeed call her from his office, and they were no more pleasant to her than Jenkins had been. The nerve of some people. They were going to be out of a job when this was done. She'd make sure of it, and she'd have that man's estate before he touched a penny of hers.

The files were set to go. She had only to pick them up and head to the courthouse in two days. One really, she told herself, as it was already late evening. Caroline decided that she'd go and get her something to eat, and put on her second best. She had a great many smart dresses, but she was saving the nicest for court.

Walking down the street, she had to be careful of her ankle. "Darn boy is going to pay for that. I should have hit him harder is what I should have done." There were people staring at her as she spoke to herself, and she told them to leave her alone. "I don't have anything to do with your beeswax—you stay out of mine."

Angry now that she'd had to get feudal with a couple of people, she got to the diner just as they were locking the door. Mabel just turned and looked at her when she told her that she was there to eat.

"We're closed." Caroline told her that it would be no problem for her to unlock the door—she was already there, after all. "We're closed. We close at seven, and its gone that time now. I'm going home. You can eat from the dumpster for all I care."

Caroline had had enough of people. Grabbing Mabel by the arm, she tossed her down the three concrete steps. And when she was down on her back, she kicked her several times and took the keys from her.

"You will feed me even if I have to hold a gun on you while you do it. Now, you'll have seen that I was trying to be nice, but when I want something, even if it's some of your nasty food, then you're to take care that I have it." Trying to help the woman up, she was dismayed to find that she was unconscious, and dropped her again. "Darn it, I just wanted to eat."

Using the keys, she entered the place and looked around for someone to feed her. Closing at seven was stupid. That was supper time, didn't they realize that? After finding the lights and turning them all on, she went to the kitchen. Of course, they'd not left anything out that someone like her could fix up.

Caroline knew how to cook. She'd never paid a person in her life to come into her home, use her things, and cook a meal that she could very well do on her own. The same with her house. She cleaned it, dusted every day, and even did her own laundry. Making her bed was something that she detested doing, but she did it anyway. A neat home, she'd always thought, was one that you could take pride in.

There were no instructions on how to turn on the stove, nor were there any for the big grill or deep fryer. Finding nothing in the refrigerator, she came out angrier than she was before. Smashing the stack of plates that was on the table, Caroline felt marginally better. So she broke every dish and glass that she found.

"It's for how they treated me. Closing the doors at seven. I bet they never do that again. When Caroline Spencer says to cook for her, that is just what she means, darn it."

There were other things to break as well. And in the walk-in refrigerator she threw the tomatoes against the walls, then used a knife on the meats that were just lying there. Cabbage and bowls of slaw were tossed around. When she walked out of there, she went into the dining area and broke anything that was breakable there.

Leaving when she felt better, Caroline dropped the keys back on Mabel as she walked by her, kicking her once more as she did so. Making her way back to the inn, she brushed off the food that had gotten on her. Nothing to eat made her cranky, and she knew that she wasn't fit to be around people when she was like that.

The grocery store was open, but not the entire thing. There was construction going on, and signs everywhere that they could see if they had what you needed. What she needed was a hot meal, and it didn't look like she was going to get one. Then it hit her. Rachel would cook for her.

She still had no idea where she lived, but that wouldn't stop her. After purchasing an apple, paying too much for it, she asked around for their home address. But again, like before, she had no luck having people tell her where her niece lived.

The police went by her while she was trying to decide what to do, and decided that she'd better get back to her room. There was no telling what that woman would tell them once she was picked up. Who decided hours like she had on the diner? Caroline would keep it open until she thought it was a reasonable time, but no one consulted her on such matters. Mores the pity.

Changing into her night dress, she sat on the rocker and wrote down every penny she'd spent. And when she was ten cents short on what she should have had in her pocket book, Caroline checked her clothing. There she found it, and a quarter.

"It's the little things like this that make a person happy." Balancing out her checkbook, even though she'd not written a single check, Caroline made herself ready for bed. "I will be happy to be done with this town. It just makes me all the more angry that things aren't going my way."

She knew that she'd have her rewards for it as soon as the trial began. Everyone would find out what a good person she was, as well as how she was going to raise David. He'd be the image of her, she thought, right down to having money in his pocket. Walking around money, she called it. Caroline was proud of that, the money she'd been able to put away. And when David was ready to take over, he'd work just as hard as she had to make himself a millionaire. Rachel would never be able to claim that, not the way she was acting.

Taking her hair down from the bun she wore it in, Caroline brushed the curls out over and over — one hundred strokes at each handful of strands. By the time she was finished, it was well past ten and she was exhausted. Braiding her long hair into a single braid, she tied it off at the end with a piece of string that she held onto for that very reason, and laid in her bed. Pulling out her notes, she added to the list of things that she was going to beat into David's head when they left here, and then added that she needed to send the bill for her dry cleaning and extra nights' stay to Rachel. It was the least she could do for all the trouble that she was causing her.

In order to rest easily, she went over her list that she'd have to get done when she got back to her home. The list was growing now, but it was mostly things that her nephew was going to have to do in order to get into her good graces. The lawn would need a good going over now that it was warmer.

Caroline had never spent any money on things that she could use for free. The lawn mower was no different. It had been left at her home by the previous owners, and she saw no reason not to keep right on using it. It had to be sharpened every year, but it worked well and built character for the person pushing it. Since there was no gasoline or electric going to the thing, she wasn't sickened by the smells either. Just plain cut grass.

"David will thank me for it when he starts building muscle instead of staying indoors all the time with some kind of game plastered to his face." She had seen the way that kids used those games when she was out. No more conversation at the table, not if they had one of those things.

Then when he turned eighteen, she'd put him in the military. She knew that was a place that would knock some sense into the boy. And she'd make sure that he went on, too, to retire from there with not just a good pension, but also money each month for her. Caroline wished every day that Mother had put Alan in one of the branches.

He'd been ready to face the world then. Not the way he was before he was murdered— Caroline would never have put up with that. No, he would have been a good man. And perhaps he might have done more with his children. Rachel was a lost cause as far as she was concerned. Nothing to show for her twenty some years on this planet.

Sleep took her, as it always did—awake one second then out the next. Her dreams were the same too. Caroline was living with her mother and things were different. She'd be running things, and her mother and her little paintings would have been in a shelter or nursing home. It didn't matter which one, so long as Mother was out of her sight. Caroline might even drive out to the house tomorrow and see what was left behind for her to get. Maybe that car. She'd wanted that car since the day that she'd seen it. Tomorrow was going to be a good day. Caroline just knew it.

~*~

Levi was helping Christian gather what he was going to need. Each time he or Ray gave him something else and explained how they'd gotten it, he would smile a little bigger. Levi got up to take the phone call when Barnes told him there was one for him.

"Levi, I'm sorry to bother you at home, but I was hoping to find your brother Jules. There's been a murder and — well, the only thing that I can call it is a break in. Though, they didn't take any money." Landon Hartman had stepped in as police chief when his wife was killed and he'd been bored. "You know that older crew of men that has coffee every morning in the diner? The ones that everyone calls the Lairs Club? Well, they were headed there when they saw her body. Called me right away. Never went in, but it wouldn't have done them a bit of good. It's a mess, son. A terrible mess. I don't know who would do something like this but a bunch of kids."

"Who was murdered?" He told him. "Mabel Spinster is dead? How? Why? You said it was kids. Do you think she walked in on it?"

"I don't know. We found her with her keys on her, and the bank bag. Nothing seemed to be taken." Levi reached for his brother, only to be told to wait. "She was beat up pretty badly, Levi. Someone kicked her around a few times as well. Best we can tell she was knocked down the stairs, and then

108

she hit her head on the steps. Might well have spooked them all off, but I'm trying my best not to jump to conclusions."

"I reached out to Jules, but so far nothing back. I'll let him know that you're looking for him." Then he thought of something. "Have you called in Tess? I know that she has a better handle on these things than any of us do, being a former cop and all."

"I'll do that. Unless you can be quicker."

Levi reached for her. After telling her what was going on and asking about Jules, Tess said she'd meet him there.

He's on a mission. I'm sorry. I really wanted some ice cream, and they don't carry any here yet. But why he didn't speak to you is worrisome, don't you think? Levi said it could be anything or nothing. *Yeah, that's what I'm hoping for too. I'll keep trying, or you can, but he might be more inclined to talk to you after today. I've been demanding,* he said.

She was laughing when he closed the connection. After telling Landon what he knew, he decided that he'd go see about it as well. Might as well all of them figure this out. He just knew in the back of his mind that Caroline had something to do with this.

After telling Ray and his brother what was going on, Levi and Ray went to the diner. She told him several times not to allow her to touch Mabel. Since she'd been gone for a little while, neither of them knew what bringing her back might be. Or if Ray even could. But he thought it was better to be safe than sorry.

The ambulance was there, as was Tess. She was dressed in a pair of sweat pants and a tee, and he could see the beginnings of her baby bump. It wouldn't be until late summer that she had the child, but he knew that she had three more babies at home. Jules's household was fun.

Dane showed up just as they were taking pictures of the inside of the place.

"It was done by a human, but at this point, I'm not sure who. I have an idea, but I don't want to jump to conclusions right now." Dane looked at Ray as she continued. "From what I'm hearing, there is a court date set up for her and you, correct?"

"Yes—tomorrow, as a matter of fact." She looked around, and Levi wondered if Ray was afraid she was nearby. "I don't know one hundred percent if it was her or not, but about ninety-nine percent. She's at the B&B."

"Yes, first thing I did was go by there, and she's still in bed. Looks like she had been all night, too. Sara can't remember what time she came in, but it was after supper." Ray asked if she'd said anything. "She didn't catch it all, but something about sending you the bill for the extra stay. I guess Sara asked her how much longer she was staying."

"She hates to spend money." Dane laughed. "What are you going to do? Bring her in for questioning? I would. If she did it, she'll be happy to tell you that she did and what her reasons were for doing it."

"I have no doubt that she will. But what I'd rather do is have her say that in front of the judge tomorrow. I know that you have a lot to lay on her door, honey, but it won't hurt one bit for us to give all we can in this. The more we can have in our corner, the longer she'll be staying in jail. By the way, did you tell anyone what I found?"

Ray glanced at Levi and said that she'd not yet. That she was saving it for the next time she spoke to Caroline. It was her ace in the hole. Dane said it was a good idea and walked away. Levi asked her about it.

"It's big and bad at the same time." She whispered in his ear what it was, and he could only stand there, shocked. "I'm trying to keep it from David too. I don't know how he'll react to this—it might not bother him at all. But it will cause so many things to be changed that I want to be right there when she hears from me what I've been able to unearth."

"Christ, Ray. That is a bombshell." She nodded, and watched as they put Mabel in the ambulance. He looked in that direction as well. "She was a sour woman most of the time. But she was well liked too. And could cook up a storm when she wanted to. I wonder what really happened here."

They walked home after that—not speaking, but lost in thought. Levi had some packing up to do, and he wanted to check on the painting too. His cock got hard just thinking about what they'd done. He was nearly to their home when his mom pulled in the driveway with Dad.

"We just heard. That poor woman. Does anyone have any idea what happened? Or why?" Levi told his dad that they were still looking into it. But so far all they knew was that it was human. "Honey, I don't want you to take this wrong, but I'm betting it's that aunt of yours. She's a creature, isn't she?"

"That is an apt description of her. A creature. From some other world too. I hope it wasn't her—I really do—but I also think it was. She could hurt someone like that and blame anyone for what she'd done."

Levi told his parents what was going on tomorrow, and that Ray had a bombshell to drop too.

"I won't ask you what it is. I'm going to be just as surprised as everyone else." He asked his mom if they had any breakfast plans. "Yes, we were thinking that we need to go into town,

111

Columbus, and do a little shopping for this street fair that's coming up. My goodness, Levi, you'd not believe the things that are going to be there for sale. Why, I've even asked for a booth to sell off some of those piece of old furniture that none of you wanted."

"Did you let Wyatt go through it?" Mom said that he'd done that last night. "I bet he took the dining room set, didn't he? I think that he's been hoping none of us would want it. He said he has memories of holidays on that sucker that he wants to keep."

"He took that, as well as your old patio furniture that you bought and didn't use. The set you have back there now, I wish I could find me a set like that." Mom looked at Dad as she continued. "Why don't we keep an eye out for that, too, while we're there? I have a mind to have someone sitting out there having tea in my new garden."

Ray was quiet while they spoke, but told them that she'd love to go into town with them. And to get breakfast. Right now, she told them she wasn't too hungry, but would be by the time they got there. They'd drive themselves in, as they wanted to see if David wanted to go. He was all up for it. Spending time with his family, he told Levi, was what life was all about. Levi was still laughing about how he'd said it as they pulled out of the driveway. This could be fun, he thought. And a chance to get away from town for a while. It wasn't hiding from her aunt, but more that they were getting out of town to forget about her. Tomorrow was going to be a hell of a day.

Breakfast was loud and filling. They lingered a while over their drinks, talking about the street fair that was in a few days. Levi had some smaller prints of his pictures that he was

112

giving away as raffle prizes, and Ray had donated a table and chairs — to fatten the pot, she said.

After deciding where to go first, Dad picked up the check, no matter how many times Levi told him that he had it, and they were off again. Ray had a list of things that she wanted to look at, and David asked for a computer. The one he had was as old as he was, he told them.

"I'm going to take some tutoring classes online. I'm still having trouble with my math." Levi asked if Brayden had been any help. "Yes. A great deal. But he is really busy with all his projects, and I hate taking him away from that. Did you know that he invents things too, Mom?"

"Yes. You should have him tell you about what he's done in Africa. I've read up on it, and the rest Dane told me about. Also, avoid talking about Vonda." David laughed, and said that he'd heard about her, from everyone. "Me too. I'm glad I didn't know her. I might have had to put her in the chipper."

They'd watched a few movies over the last few days. One was about a place in the Dakotas about a kidnapping gone wrong. It frightened him just a little when David asked if Dane had done anything like that. While he didn't have an answer for him, Levi was slightly afraid to ask her about it too. So of late, they'd all been talking about different parts of the movie. Mostly the gory stuff.

Having dinner after they'd gotten much more than they had room for, he was glad that Colton and Hailey were in town to give them a hand. Taking them to dinner with them was payment enough, he told them, and Colton told him what he'd found out at the hospital.

"They're closing down a hospital in one of the bigger cities in Ohio. They have several in that area now, but this one is a newly remodeled updated place." David asked what that might do for the other hospitals and the people working there. "They're being transferred. Not a lot of them are happy about the moves, either. But since they need to have a job, they're going to do it. Some of them have been at the other hospital for over thirty years. That's a long time to suddenly just be told you no longer work someplace."

"I've been thinking a great deal about what I want to be when I go to college. And while I have a great deal to learn about a lot of things, I've decided that I love what Colton does. He gets into the mind of people and helps them." Colton told David that it didn't always work out. "Yes, I'm aware of that too. I did some research on everything that you guys do, including my aunts, and while I'd love to be like the women, I think I'd live longer if I stuck with an office job. You guys are scary."

"We protect everyone we love, however." David hugged Hailey, and she hugged him back. "And you, my dear boy, are going to live forever. Both of you will, thanks to the magic that we all share. I don't know if anyone told you that or not, but once you hit a certain age—I have no idea what that might be—you'll not age, nor will you die. So if you want, you can try out all of the things you wish, and figure out what you wish to do."

Ray looked at Levi, then at Hailey. "Is this true?" Hailey nodded. "Holy fuck balls, I'm going to have some fun now."

They were all laughing as they left for home. Levi was surprised that Mom didn't hush Ray. But then, she seemed as shocked as the rest of them were.

Chapter 9

Ray watched the people in the courtroom. There were a lot more than she had thought there would be. It wasn't like Caroline was known much around town. But then, she had been making herself a nuisance since she arrived. Ray didn't want to think about the fact that she had more than likely killed that poor woman.

"What have I missed?" Levi had worked all night so that he could be here today with her. He looked a little tired. "I'll be fine. I can see the worry in your eyes. But when the muse hits me with something, I have to work."

"I understand that too. But couldn't Muse be a little more timely?" He laughed, and people turned to look at him. "She looks like she has already won, doesn't she?"

Caroline was sitting next to her attorney, Paul Jenkins, staring at the dais. The smile on her face was simple—just a smile—but it was the look around her eyes when she glanced at her that scared her a bit. Ray asked again if she'd been checked for a gun.

"I promise you, all is well. And even her purse was looked into. She's not armed." It still worried her.

Ray stood up when everyone else did when the judge entered the room. Christian had asked that she not sit with him up front. He was concerned that it would rile up Caroline before the trial began.

"I understand the necessity of this seating arrangement, Mr. Stanton, but I have seen your ugly mug on several occasions. Do you think you could talk Mrs. Stanton into sitting closer? I like a pretty face as much as the next man." While the courtroom twittered a little in laughter, Ray made her way up. "David Stanton, come here as well, if you please."

"He's a minor, sir."

Judge Black just waved him forward, and he sat with her too. Ray could almost feel that Caroline had turned and looked at them. Her evilness felt as if it were boring into her flesh. Ray was ready to say that she'd not be able to sit there when Judge Black cleared his throat.

"I want to make one thing clear right now, ladies and gentlemen of the court. That would include those that are sitting right here. I want you to remain civil to one another, and that means if you can't look at someone without disdain, then you will be blindfolded. I will do it. I have no problem with that whatsoever, Ms. Spencer." Caroline opened her mouth, to no doubt say something nasty. "And tape over your mouth will happen if the next words out of your mouth aren't 'yes, your honor, I'll keep it nice.'"

She said nothing. But if her lips were any tighter together, Ray thought for sure she would not be able to unhinge her jaws. However, it must have worked. The feelings that she'd been getting before were no longer as bad.

116

"All right then, Mr. Jenkins, state your case and let's get this pony and dog show started. I, for one, am ready to enjoy the sunshine."

Jenkins stood up, and Ray watched him as he approached the judge. When asked, Christian joined them.

After a few minutes of talking, mostly laughter, the two attorneys sat down, then the judge looked over the paperwork that Ray hadn't noticed being handed to him. Judge Black looked up at Caroline a few times while looking at the paper, but he didn't say anything. Christian said this was about another matter, and that it wasn't against her.

"Ms. Spencer, Mr. Jenkins has also filed a complaint against you and your estate that says that you are in arrears of about forty thousand dollars to his firm. And in accordance to the contract that you signed with him when he first became your attorney, he will be the first in line to get his funds when you're sent to prison. If you're sent there." Caroline stood up. "You can speak, ma'am. But it had better be an explanation as to why you've not paid him."

"He charges me four hundred dollars an hour. To talk on the telephone. Four hundred dollars an hour is entirely too much for a simple conversation. I pay him when I get a bill, but only what I deem he is worth. And as far as I can see, he shouldn't even be making minimum wage from me." The judge said that it didn't work that way. "I don't care what his rules are. I know the value of money, more than some people do. And I will not waste my money on an upstart that claims to be that smart."

"I see. Well, he is stating this for the record, just so you know. First of all, he will be getting his money. And secondly, however this trial ends, he is no longer going to be your attorney. He will not defend you if you decide to appeal, either." She said that if he did his job, then she'd not need to appeal. "Be that as it may, you're on your own on any charges brought against you that are out of the realm of this lawsuit you have against Mrs. Stanton."

"She might be married, sir, but I do not choose to acknowledge it. I am her elder, and I have not given anyone permission to marry. I'll call her what her dearly departed father called her, Rachel Spencer." Judge Black just shook his head. "I'd like it known that she has adopted that boy when he was to come to me, according to my brother."

"We'll get to all your claims. You hired your attorney for this, let him do the talking." Judge Black slammed down his gavel when she stood up again. "Ms. Spencer, this court will have this trial today even if I have to have you arrested on contempt of court. Now, I'm asking you nicely, again, to sit down and shut the hell up."

Caroline took the stand a few minutes later. Ray pulled the pad of paper she'd brought with her to start making notes on what she said. Most of it was going to be lies, but she wanted to be able to have an answer for each of her points against her. Ray was to about number ten when she paused to look at her aunt as she spoke.

"...so every time I visited my mother, she told me how Rachel had come to the house and had taken all her valuables away. And even after her death, there she was, taking every last piece of my childhood, and that of my brother, away without giving us a single thing." Mr. Jenkins asked about the reading of the will. "My mother left me her treasured seeds, the ones that she'd been saving for me for decades. I have intentions of planting them, just so I have the memories of her."

All lies. Ray had the seeds that had been sent to her when Caroline had been read the will. Caroline had tossed them into the trash can as she left, pissed because that was all she'd left her. Christian had had her bring them with her today. She was glad now that he was a smart attorney.

Caroline also went on about how the house was in such disrepair, and that since her mother was watching over David for Rachel, she could have at least fixed the roof for her. That should be little money compared to the millions she professed to have. As it was now, Caroline was going to have to sell off some of the valuables that were still left in the barn to get the house back up to living standards.

There wouldn't be any way she was going to be able to get the house back up to living standards, but it wasn't Ray's turn. If there was even going to be a turn for her to sit in front of the courtroom. When she heard her name, she looked up and then around, and noticed that everyone was staring at her. Asking Christian what she'd done now, he smiled at her. It was full of humor. Before he could answer her, Caroline spoke again.

"Just look at her. Sitting there making up little stories so she can sell them off. I won't have her telling a thing about me. I will have to sue her if any of her stories come out and they're about me. You tell her that. I won't have it." The stomping of her foot had a few people in the courtroom snickering, and that set Caroline off too. "What are you laughing about? You sit here and behave, or I shall have you all removed from here. I will not have people laughing at me behind my back."

"If you don't mind, I'm in charge, Ms. Spencer. And I won't tell you that again." Apparently in Ray's note-taking at several points this morning, she'd missed Judge Black telling Caroline he was the man in charge. "Now, proceed. And Ms. Spencer, remember, you're on thin ice with me already. Don't be pulling any more of your wounded hero crap either. I know a great deal about you."

"I have no idea what you're talking about. And if you can't say anything civil to me, why, just keep your mouth shut." Judge Blake looked shocked, as did the rest of the people there. "Now, where was I? Oh, I was telling everyone what a horrid grandchild Rachel is. You should see some of the outlandish things that she's been doing since my dear mother passed. Unspeakable. And she flaunts around like she's a floozy or something."

Christian asked to speak and his request was granted. He looked right at Caroline, and it made Ray wish she could see her face when she sputtered and sat back further on her chair.

"Your Honor, I think that Ms. Spencer has said enough regarding her opinion of Mrs. Stanton. And she is way off track of what this hearing is about. She is claiming that my client went against the wishes of her grandmother and father. Not to mention, she's put herself up on a pedestal so high that if she was to fall off, she'd surely break her neck." Caroline stood up, then sat when Christian told her to. Then he continued. "I'm like you, sir. I'd like to finish this so we can get outside."

"I agree. Ms. Spencer. If you are done prattling on about how you're the next to be canonized as a saint, then I'd like to allow this to go forward." When asked if he had anything to say to this, Mr. Jenkins said he was finished. While Ray had an idea what he meant, he didn't say anything to help his client along. "Go ahead, Mr. Stanton, have your questions with her."

"You said that you visited your mother recently. Can you narrow that down for me? I know that it would have been before her death, of course. But can you tell me if it was a week? Two? It would help me a great deal." She answered him. "The day before. Thank you. Have you been out to the house since her passing?"

"Yes, just the other day, as a matter of fact. I picked some of her favorite flowers that were in full bloom around the front door to her house. She had the prettiest flowers all over her yard, and even though she has passed, they're still just as lovely. I put them on her grave on the way home from there. Why?"

~*~

Christian handed out the eight by tens that he'd taken of the house the day after they'd gotten the last of their things out. The house had been demolished. And the other day when he'd been out, there were small sprouts of corn coming up. Not a single flower in sight.

"These flowers that you picked. Can you tell me where they might have been? Because I know for a fact that the house and lands surrounding it were sold off about two months before Alma's passing. Mrs. Ray Stanton sold it all to the neighbor to use as more field for him." Caroline asked what right she had to do that. "She's been the sole owner of the property for the last fifteen years. The taxes were in arrears, as well as the house needed a new roof and windows. At the time Ray bought it from her grandmother, she'd not paid the taxes in a decade or so. It was a mutual agreement between the two of them. And Alma could live there, without any cost to her — that would include her utilities. When Alma passed away, less than twenty-four hours after her death the house and barn were taken down. So, again, I asked you where you picked your mothers favorite flowers."

"I might have missed the days, that's all." Christian was going to leave that for now. "I want to know when I'm going to be able to take my nephew home with me. My brother left instructions that I was to get David if he passed away before I did. And there wasn't any other interpretation of that statement. I'm going to take him home with me and beat him into submission, enough to learn what he needs to be a successful man."

"When you say you're going to beat him into submission, you mean that quite literally, don't you?" Caroline asked him what he meant. "You *will* beat him. And in turn, you plan on breaking him so that he does exactly what you wish of him. Is that correct?"

"Yes. I'm a firm believer in 'spare the rod spoil the child.' Sometimes you must get a child's attention before he begins to learn anything." Christian asked her what was her choice of weapon. "I have a belt that my father used. Not on me, not a great deal, but he did. What is the point of all this? I don't believe that your mother beat you enough, young man."

"You'd be surprised. Tell me, what are your plans for David, after you beat him into submission?" Again, she asked him what he meant. He had a feeling that she understood him, but was thinking of her answer before she spoke. "You must have a plan. What is it?"

"He will have good grades, or I will know the reason why. When he's old enough to be signed up, I'll sign him up for one of the military branches. That will make a man out of him quicker than I could. And much better than his sister could ever imagine doing. And if you're thinking of asking me, I'll have his pay directed to me. I'll set him up in a nice home close to me so that I can make sure that he continues with the way I want things to go." Christian asked her if David had any say over his life. "No. I find that men, all men, are only out for one thing, and he'll not have any sex unless I approve of the woman."

"Are you going to stand over them and make sure he does that to your liking as well? You more than likely only approve of the missionary position, don't you?" She told him to shut his dirty mouth. "Dirty mouth? No, I'm just pointing out that you're molding David into the creature you want him to be. Is it because you missed out on doing those sorts of things to your own son?"

This was where he'd been heading, and she'd followed him right down the path, just like he'd known she would. When she just stared at him, anger rolling off her in buckets, Christian asked her again.

"I haven't any idea what you're talking about, young man. I'm not a married woman. I have no children." She glared harder. "You will stop this sort of talk right this minute, or so help me, you're going to regret it."

"You see, that's where you're wrong. On a great many things, Caroline. I won't stop with this line of questioning, and I won't regret a thing when I'm finished." He smiled at her as he picked up his file that was on the table. "Now, are you planning to beat David into the sort of person you didn't get to direct your own son into? Surely you remember carrying your son for nine months and giving birth. I don't think that would be something you'd forget easily."

"I told you to stop talking about that. That is none of

your business, and as I stated, I do not have a son." Christian nodded and sat on the corner of the desk, waiting for her to talk more. One thing he'd learned about criminals was, they hated silence and had to fill it. "I do not have a son. I have a brother. Perhaps you're just a hiney hole and can't keep your nose out of someone else's business. Now, I told you to shut up about this, and I'm not kidding you. Stop talking about my life."

"This lie you've been telling. It's not just affecting your life, as you said, but everyone's. Your wonderful mother raised your child when you decided that you didn't want to give it up. Never once in all the years did you help her with Alan, did you? You wouldn't babysit, wouldn't get up in the middle of the night with him. As far as myself and others see this, it just goes to show what sort of mother you would be to your grandson, David." She told him to shut up. It was louder this time, and she slammed her hands down on the railing in front of her. "Then, because of your lies, all the paperwork that you had forged, it's not valid. Alan called you his sister, which you are not. By the way, when you're forging records, you should really check which courthouse your mother filed Alan's birth certificate in. It helped us to have her Bible. It has all sorts of information in it. Were you aware of that?"

"I'm telling you right now, if you don't shut up, I'm going to permanently shut you up. Now, I want brother's child. I want you to tell them, that slut, to give over what is mine." He said she didn't have anything that belonged to her. "Bring me that Bible, too. I'm not going to have that thing lingering around telling lies on me. My mother had no right to do this to me. She was a horror of a person that I should have killed long ago."

"Ms. Spencer, you're not telling the truth, now are you? It's true that you aren't the sister to Alan Spencer, but his mother, isn't it?" Christian handed copies of the original birth certificate to the judge and to Mr. Jenkins. "So in that vein of information, you aren't the aunt of Mrs. Spencer Stanton, nor her brother, David Spencer Stanton. But their grandmother."

Christian was enjoying himself. It had been a long time since he'd had such a slam dunk trial that he could stretch out to have fun with. When she told him he was a liar, he handed an affidavit that was from the hospital where she'd given birth at seventeen.

"This is from not just the hospital, but also the attending doctor. I was surprised to find him still alive, to be honest. You have a habit of killing off those that you feel has wronged you, don't you?" He handed around the copies of the police records that had been tucked away, with money amounts that had exchanged hands in a way to make things quiet. "The father of your son, Alan, he knew nothing about the child, did he? After a single night of debauchery, you murdered him, didn't you, Caroline? And *his* daddy never found out any of it, either—not of you killing his son, nor hiding away his only grandchild."

"I'm not talking to you anymore. I'm going home." Caroline looked at Ray. "Have him packed within the hour. I'm not going to pursue my mother's things. I just want him and I'll be done with you."

"Sit down." Christian had her flopping down so hard that she snapped her teeth together. "You killed Mabel too, didn't you? Murdered her because she was closing up her diner and you wanted something to eat. Because when Caroline Spencer wants something, you don't care what the consequences are to those that are in your way. Isn't that right?"

"Who closes their doors at seven o'clock? No one does. And what would it have cost her to go in and make me some dinner? Nothing. I didn't kill her. When I knocked her around a bit, she hit her head on the steps. She should have just done what I wanted." Christian didn't expect her to give in so easily. Then she looked at Ray when she stood up. "I haven't done anything to you yet, Rachel, not like I've always wanted to do. Now that I have no one holding me back, I'll make sure that I make up for all the times that I had to hold back. You can thank your father for that. He was always whining about how you were just too pretty for me to hurt in the face. To me, that would have been the first thing that I'd have ripped from your smirking face."

"I didn't do anything wrong to warrant any of the treatment that you gave to me. Nor did David. You hurt us." Caroline said of course she did. It was her duty. "Duty? How is it a duty to beat your own grandchildren? How do you suppose it's a job for you to tie us up and set a fire close enough to our flesh that we'd blister badly?"

"You lived, more's the pity."

Christian thought it had gone on long enough. That Caroline had given them enough to have her arrested and put away. But after one look at Judge Black shaking his head no, Christian sat back down on the table.

Christian reached out to Levi and told him how sorry he was that Ray was being hurt.

She needs this as much as you do to arrest her. Finding out the truth is what she needed, not half ones. I have her, Christian, but I do thank you for being concerned.

Christian listened to Caroline basically confess what all

she'd done to Rachel and David.

"David was still trainable, I told Alan. We could mold him into any sort of person we wanted. But he had to be smart, which we all know that he's not. He also had to be loyal. David was, but to the wrong person. Alan wasn't firm enough. Beating you both, that was too much fun for him. And when we killed your mother, I knew that it was time for me to step in."

"Yes, I suppose you won something when you smothered her. Or so you thought. But you didn't, did you? I'm a better person than you ever dreamed of being. And now you're going to pay for that too." Caroline huffed and asked Rachel if she would like to die in her sleep too. "You think you can take me on, old woman? Give it your best shot."

"Oh, I'll win in the end. I always do. I would have killed you too had I been able. Your grandmother as well. But she, too, was too sly for us. Bouncing back on her feet better than we did. Then you started to protect them both. I hated you even more for that." Ray didn't back down, nor did he run, like he might have had he just been told that someone in his family killed his mother. "But we got you too, didn't we, Rachel? And now that you're all alone, I'm going to get you for my son."

"How could you be so heinous? You plotted the demise of not just our mother, but other people too. What did you hope to gain from all this?" He loved the way her mind was thinking, and wondered if Dane was feeding her what to say. "I asked you a question, Caroline. What on earth did you hope to gain by killing my mother? And my grandma?"

"I'll tell you. We were just happy to be he and I. Of course, he had no idea that I was his mother. And I haven't any idea how you figured that out. But I will. And when I leave here—and you can bet on that too—when I leave here, I'm going to take all that belongs to me. As my mother's only child, I'm entitled to all that she had. And who do you think will be hanging around once you're gone to dust?" Ray asked her why she wanted David so badly. "Where Alan didn't beat the boy enough, I had to do it. And I did until you started getting in the way. But you can bet that I will finish what we started. David will be just what I want. A star pupil."

"A star pupil at what?" Caroline only just then seemed to understand what she was doing. She became this spinster looking woman, something that he'd known she looked like, but had never noticed. Her head bowed down. Even her face seemed to have wrinkled more. "You are afraid to answer me, aren't you? You're afraid that I'll thwart your plans. And I will too. I'll protect my brother better than you did your own son."

"Whore."

The word was screamed across the room at Ray. And when Caroline stood up, making her way to Ray, David stepped in front of her just as Caroline pulled a gun from her dress pocket and fired.

Chapter 10

Ray held her brother as he slid to the floor. There wasn't time to think, so she didn't. *Save David, save David*, was the only thought that ran through her brain, blocking out every other person and noise going on in the courtroom.

"David, you have to look at me." Blood was coming from his mouth when he smiled at her. The bullet had entered his chest, and she knew that if it hadn't hit his heart, then it was very close. "Listen to me. You need to look at me so that I know that you understand what I'm doing."

"I love you, Ray-Ray. I didn't want you to die. Not when you're so happy." She saw her tear drop on his cheek. "I do love you and Levi. You're so wonderful together."

"Listen to me, you little shit. You are not going to die. Do you hear me?" He laughed, and then coughed up some blood. "You die and I'll turn you over to Caroline. I will."

She put her hand over his wound. Blood filled the area between her fingers. And when a warm hand laid over hers, she knew who it was. Levi was there. The heat that radiated

129

from his hand gave her a sense of love and understanding. Ray told her brother to look at her.

"Remember when I took you and Grandma to that amusement park? I swear she was still going when I was ready to drop. But she would drag you along to each of those rollercoasters like she had to ride them all five times each to get her money's worth." He asked her if she really had won the tickets. "You know that I didn't. I only wanted her to be able to go with us. And she wouldn't let me spend the money on her if I did it any other way."

"She knew." Ray asked David how did she know. "She said that when you win something, it's in twos. Two or four, or sometimes six if the place is cheap. You don't win three."

"Grandma was always too smart for her britches." David was getting weaker, and she could hear the ambulance way off in the distance. "David, don't leave me alone here. You're my brother, and I can't think of life without you here."

"Son. I'm son." She nodded and told him to keep his eyes open. "I don't want to die either, Ray-Ray. Love you. I wish Grandma was here to take me with her."

Ray cried harder, the tears making it difficult for her to see. And when the medics came to take over, she was backed away by Levi. The four men dressed in bright yellow weren't going to be any better at saving her brother than she had been.

As he was loaded into the ambulance, she asked to go too. They told her that they needed to keep working on him, that Doctor Stanton was going to be waiting at the other end to operate on him. The ambulance went screaming off into the setting sun, and she was left standing there with blood all over her hands and dress, and David's tie he'd taken off at some point.

No one said a word as they drove to the hospital. Levi wasn't driving, but Brayden was. Ray didn't think that anyone could drive any worse than Dane, but she was wrong. All she could think about was that Dane had taught Brayden how to drive like he had a death wish, and sidewalks were only meant to be there if the road was too busy.

When they arrived, David was already in surgery. The nurse on staff said that it didn't look good, but they would try all they could. Sitting down, then standing again when Hailey took her hand, they were headed to the sunshine ward. Ray hadn't any idea what that meant, but was glad for the distraction.

"The nursery always has been a place I can go and feel better about life in general. And since I'm with you, they'll let you hold one if you want." Ray shook her head. "Suit yourself, but you're missing a great opportunity to feel really good."

As soon as they were let into the large area, Ray had no choice but to hold an infant when one was shoved into her arms. Apparently the nursery was full to capacity, and they were short-staffed as well. Holding the little girl in her arms, she was not only given a diaper and wipes, but a bottle too. It was the tiniest thing she'd ever seen.

The diaper was wet but not terribly so. Removing it shown her that the baby had bruises along her legs and right arm. Asking what might have happened, Hailey told her that she'd let her know when they were seated. Sitting in the oversized rocker, Ray put the bottle to the baby's mouth and waited for her to latch on, while Hailey made herself comfortable with the one she had.

"The family was in a car accident. And I don't want you to think that this was not a horrible thing, because it was.

131

But, for this little girl, it was a blessing too." Ray waited for her to continue. "The mother was being beaten daily, by the drunkard prick who fathered the child. He was killed in the accident, leaving mother and daughter thankfully alone in this world."

"Will they be all right?"

While Hailey, who could read people well, thought about her answer, Ray did some thinking of her own. She wanted a child. It didn't matter to her what sex the baby was, she just wanted to have a child with Levi. Hailey said her name, and Ray had a feeling it wasn't the first time.

"Cover up her leg." It was whispered in a way that had Ray covering her legs right away. "I'm assuming that you healed her ribs too? And with that, I had to do a follow up appointment. Were you aware that I can have children now as well?"

"I didn't know. But I'm very happy for you both. I don't know about her ribs. I can only assume so." Ray looked at her small ribcage that had been nasty shades of blue and black before she'd fed her. "What do I do? I don't want anyone to know what I've done."

"They know some of what we can do, so the nurses here on staff will only thank you. But there is a person standing outside the room there that I think is related to the baby." Ray didn't look, but asked her who it was. "Grandmother. I didn't want her to see how the bruises were fading while it was happening. She's going to be very helpful in their new life, I think."

Rocking two more babies after the first one, Ray was getting to be good at changing diapers too. The staff brought in two more newborns while she and Hailey were helping out. Twins were put in the same buggy, as they called them, because there were no more of them left to fill.

The little hats, she'd found out, were donated by the local nursing home. The women and men that could would work on them at arts and crafts, and when a child was fitted with one of them, a picture would be sent to the one who made it. Nurse Valery said it made their day, and kept the babies warm while in the hospital.

"We have so much outside help that it makes things better for us here, even when we're this busy. Some of the nursing students will come in a couple of times a week and help out when we need them. And these nice bags that we send home with each new parent are filled by another nursing home that also knits or crochets baby blankets." The nurse showed her what was in the medium sized bag. "They put the blanket, brush and comb set, wipes, and diapers in it with all the coupons we're given. And another hat. When a baby is ready to leave us, we put in the formula that they're using, as well as the things that the infant had been using here. The most useful thing we toss in besides the formula is a baby thermometer."

"Do you get donations on all this? Or is the hospital footing the bill?" She was told it was a lot of donations, but not nearly enough. The hospital was going to cut them soon. "Is there a foundation that is set up for this sort of thing?"

"Not that I'm aware of. I think that all the donations that come in for us to use are distributed all over the hospital, for people with no income or insurance kind of things. Also, a little bit of money goes toward a fund that the area florist put together, to send flowers to someone who might not have anyone around to bring them some. I used to work the geriatric floor, and you'd not believe how a little bouquet of flowers can brighten someone's day."

Ray's mind was working on how to set up donations for the nursery, and also for the funding for necessary surgical funding. Anything and everything that didn't allow her to think of her brother. Nor her aunt. She supposed now she could call her Grandma, but decided to stick to just calling her by her given name. It was easier on her heart that way.

The next baby she was given was one that was being brought down off of drugs. Her mother had taken them all through her pregnancy, and now the baby was just as dependent on them as she'd been. Unfortunately for the child, his little body was having a worse time now that he wasn't getting his daily fix through Mom.

When he'd taken all she could get him to drink, she held him tightly to her breast and spoke to him. Mostly it was to tell him what she had been doing since she'd arrived, and how he was the most handsome of all the babies she'd seen today. Then she whispered to him not to tell any of the others, they'd be so jealous. Just silly things like that.

"I have a little brother. He's almost seventeen now." She hurt for him, both of the little boys. "He'd have a fit if he knew that I was calling him a boy. But there is this other wonderful woman that calls her sons boys, and they're all as big as houses. Did anyone ever read you *The Big Red Dog*? I'll make sure you get a copy."

Another thing to add to her list was books. Each child would get a book to take home with them. Their first of many things that they'd see as they grew up. Ray asked the little man in her arms if he'd like a baby book, one he could show off to his girlfriend when he started dating.

There was a noise behind her, but she didn't turn.

Monitors had been going off for the last few minutes, and Ray had learned to shut them out. When the baby closed his eyes she continuing rocking him, knowing deep in her heart that he'd passed away. The nurse told her that he had all kinds of things wrong with him physically, as well as more than likely mentally. All they could do now was give him some comfort while he was there.

"When you're up there in Heaven, young man, I want you to look for my grandma. Her name is Alma Spencer. She's a hoot, and makes the best strawberry jam in the world." Ray wiped at her tears as she kept talking to the baby. "She gives the best hugs too. Even when you don't think you need one, she can wrap you up in her arms and you feel like you can do just about anything, they're that good."

The nurse told her it was time and took the baby from her. She was as gentle with him as she had been when he was alive. And Ray noticed that she spoke to him too, telling him what was going to happen to him and what he was going to see when he left there. Whatever it was, Ray thought, she hoped that it was going to be a better place than he had had here.

Ray did feel better as she made her way to the waiting room with the others. The baby had been loved before he'd passed on. Another had been healed for the trip home, and a lot of bellies were full and butts dried. She'd have to thank Hailey for this. Ray hadn't been able to think about how she not been able to save David. She wanted him to be healed too.

When she got off the elevator, Ray knew that something was wrong.

"I'm sorry, Ray."

Levi held her as she collapsed. He was still talking, but

she couldn't hear him anymore. It was too much. She'd lost entirely too much, and her heart could no longer take it.

~*~

Today was Bryn's last day driving a school bus. Not that she was going to miss the job. In actuality, she hated it—overprivileged children being carted to school in what amounted to a school bus sized limo. There were even hook ups at each reclining seat if they needed to charge up one of their expensive electronic devices.

There was even bulletproof glass all around them in the event that someone wanted to try and take the bus with them on it. A locking device would kick in when she pressed a button on her dashboard. The air conditioning for summer, and the heat for winter, would blow her away. And if one of the students was not at the stop when she arrived, she was to call into the house and ask the butler or maid that answered if they were coming in today. Bryn knew better than to just assume with these people.

Her next charge was coming down the walk, doing something on her phone, when she got to her stop. This kid, this girl, was the worst of the worst. She had a clique of friends that would spit in someone's face if Porsche Humphrey, her name, told them to. Bryn had seen it happen, and nothing had ever come of it. Not that it had happened to her, but she had been the reporting personnel. They had told her that girls will fight, and it's not that big of a deal. Well, she thought it was. Especially since if you spit on a cop, you went to jail. These people, she figured out, were above such things as rules and laws.

When Porsche finally got on the bus, she stopped long enough to look Bryn over. Bryn had stopped dressing to impress a long time ago. The only person that ever noticed her clothing was this girl, and she usually turned her nose up at everything she wore.

Bryn closed the doors after the girl was seated, but she paused in driving off when a man came running out of the house toward the bus.

"Do not wait for him. I don't want whatever it is he has." Bryn just looked at the young girl in the overhead mirror and waited. "Did you hear what I told you? I said to go on."

"You said not to wait for him. I'm sure you didn't tell me to go on. And I'm waiting for him because it's my job to do so. Now, would you please come up here and see what he has for you?"

Porsche stomped to the front of the bus when Bryn opened the door for the man. He was out of breath, and seemed to be holding his chest hard. She asked him if he was all right. Before he could answer her, however, Porsche told her that it was none of her business if he was or wasn't.

Snatching the large padded envelope from the man, Porsche dismissed him by turning her back toward them both and flouncing to her seat. Bryn asked the man again if he was all right. He looked a little better, and was smiling now.

"Yes, thank you. Everything is going to be all right now."

She thought that was a strange thing to say, but closed the door and made sure that her charge was in her seat. As he made his way back to the big mansion, Bryn put the bus in gear and moved on.

There were a few more stops to be made before she was finished for the day. It was the last day of school for these kids, and Bryn was going to turn in her notice when she got to the garage. It was going to be a nice summer for her; her vacation was all planned out.

Sleep late, eat whatever she wanted. Job hunt, and she was going to finally get her doctorate's degree in languages. She just needed to take the test and she'd be looking at a better income. Which also meant that she'd be able to afford a place that was better than where she lived now, plus a car that actually ran, which she only kept in case she was ever homeless again. That wasn't a thing that happened a great deal. But books came before rent, because Bryn knew that it would pay off in the end. She'd be Bryn Dell MacKenzie when she was finished.

Bryn watched the next kid coming down the front walkway from his home. He dropped his paperwork, and as it spread all over the lawn, he looked at her as if it were all her fault. Over-indulged fucking little shit. She sat there for two minutes hoping he'd just get it himself, but he stood there, tapping his foot until she got the message that she was to come and get them for him.

Putting the bus in park, she told the kids she'd be back. Nothing would make her want to do this job for another year. Not even if they paid her ten times what she was paid now — which was pretty good.

Bryn got out of the bus and was headed toward him when she was suddenly thrown forward. It took her a moment to realize that she'd not been attacked from behind, nor had she been hit by a car — both things seemed to come to her at once. Then she thought that one of the kids would have to move up off their expensive, overdone asses before that could happen, and she just laid on the ground.

Her head was buzzing and she couldn't hear anything but a loud high pitched whine that made her think of when she'd been in the service. Jets going over head and dropping God knew what to the ground. While she had been too hot earlier—it was the end of May—she was now freezing. Shivering too.

There were other sounds too, ones that her fuddled mind couldn't make out, nor make sense of. Bryn looked up only to be sick with the pain of moving. Closing her eyes, she tried to think. But she was in so much pain all over her body that she didn't do that for long. She knew that she had to move; it was pounding in her head that she had to get up, get going before whatever had hit her came back.

Sitting up, she looked around and tried her best to figure out what had happened to her. Looking at the street, her confused mind took a few seconds to make her realize what she was really seeing. The bus was gone. No, that wasn't right. It was there, but it was on fire. The roof of it was burning, the name of the school was melting away. The front and side windows that they told her could withstand a gunshot were gone, as was the entire back end where the wheels had once been.

Trying to stand, Bryn staggered to it, only to be pushed back by the heat. It wasn't just hot, it was volcanic hot—much too hot for her, but she moved forward. The kids, her mind screamed at her. Those were her charges on the bus. Bryn knew that she had to save them. Or, as many as she could.

Getting on the bus proved to be much harder than she thought it should have been. The doors were blown into the hedges in the next house's yard. The steps were sticky with the melting rubber. But she was able to get on it.

Bryn tried not to look beyond the first child she came to. He was alive, but was screaming at her to help him. He was

139

burning hot, his clothing too, and when he touched her, she felt his fingers burn marks into her skin. Pulling him out of the seat as best she could, Bryn dragged him down the stairs and to the ground near the walkway at the house. One down and four to go.

The second person she came across was alive as well, but he looked bad. Most of his face had been burnt, and all his hair was gone. Patting out the fire that was still burning on his pants, she did the same to him, dragging him to the walk. Then she had to rest.

The heat and her headache were making her slow. Bryn didn't know if she could go in there again, pull another child from the bus. What if she were to fail? Bryn thought they'd fire her, and not give her the pension she had coming.

"What are you doing? Get the rest of them off there."

Nodding, Bryn moved toward the bus again. The man behind her was screaming into a cell phone — or at her, she couldn't tell. Bryn hoped he was calling for help, or at the very least the police.

The third person was dead. Whatever had blown in the bus had taken most of her chest out. Bryn couldn't drag the person out, not in the shape they were in, so she moved to the next two people — Porsche and her best friend. They too were dead.

Her mind would not take in how bad they looked. Most of Porsche was simply gone. The only thing that would have been able to tell Bryn who it was, if she didn't know where the girl sat every day, was her bookbag and a cell phone. The rest of her, and the girl next to her, were nothing but splatters of blood and other parts that were not something Bryn wanted to name.

Bryn was in such pain now that she had to sit down on the floor of what was left of the bus. The fire was still burning, but it didn't matter to her. She was hurting, and couldn't breathe around the pain any longer. Her head was spinning, and she was sick. Looking down at her belly, she was terrified when she saw that there was a large piece of blood covered metal sticking out of her. Closing her eyes, she tried to think how she was going to get off here, with the three children.

Just as she was going to just drag out their burnt bodies, someone touched her. Bryn didn't have any idea what she'd been thinking, or if she had been, but she screamed when he loomed over her. She told the aberration to leave her kids alone.

"I'm Steward, the CO of this parish. I'm going to get you out to safety." She said she couldn't leave the kids. "Come on now, honey. They're too far gone for you to save."

"They won't care. These children are in my care, and I have to see to their needs before my own." He asked her if she was serous. "It's in the manual. They make you sign it. Can you imagine that? I have to make sure that I bring them home at night, or I could lose my job."

"Miss, if I get you off here, I can come back for the bodies with help." Shaking her head, she was sick again and leaned back on the seat behind her. "All right then. You just sit right there and I'll see what I can do."

She knew that she had passed out, and Bryn also knew that she was losing a great deal of blood. If she made it out of this, she'd bet anything that not only would she lose her job, but that someone would blame her for this. She was going to quit anyway, but she didn't want to be blamed for what had happened here. Three dead children, and all the damage was going to be more than she could handle. Bryn didn't know if she could handle it now.

The next time she opened her eyes, she saw a man looming over her again. He might have said his name, but she was too busy screaming her head off. The pain was certainly making itself known to her now. All she could do was hurt, and when she felt someone take her arm, she knew that they were giving her something to shut her up. Fighting against it as best she could, Bryn grabbed the man's arm and tried to speak.

Cuir fios gu Doctor Stanton, mas e do thoil e? Bryn's mind screamed at her when she realized what she'd done. "Please, call Doctor Stanton for me. He'll help me. Call him for me."

"All right. Let the pain medicines take you under and we'll take care of it."

But she knew he wouldn't. She was out of her mind in pain, and she might, in his mind, have caused the explosion. Soon, however, the meds took her pain away, and she was able to fight through the pain enough to see a man dressed in a uniform close to her.

She couldn't move enough to reach out and touch him—couldn't make her hands work at all. Her lips weren't cooperating either. But when he turned to look at her, Bryn felt something move over her, something that she was afraid of.

"My doctor, could you call him?" He nodded but didn't speak. "His name is Doctor Stanton. I'm fading fast here. So if you're not going to do it, please tell me."

"Do you have enough left in you to tell me the number?" Lying back on the pillow, the man said her name. "Bryn? Can you tell me the number?"

She was ill now with the meds and her pain. They were

moving her; the lights above her were blinking off and on as she moved under them. The man, whoever he was, still walked with them. Wherever they were taking her, the man was being asked to wait outside.

The argument must have been quick, because before she could think how it had happened, the officer was with her, but he was dressed as an angel. Bryn shook her head mentally. Angels? Instead, she worked her mouth hard to get enough spit in it to work. She would swear for as long as she lived that she saw him as a cat, a cougar, just before he spoke again.

"Bryn, honey, tell me his number. Then they'll take the pain away." It was then that she realized that he was speaking to her in Gaelic. "What's his number?"

She gave it to him just as she was feeling woozy again. Even trying to fight it this time, she knew it was a lost cause. But her friend, he would save her. He'd come here, get her out of the hospital, and put her someplace safe. Because as surely as she was laying here, Bryn knew that as soon as this this hit the papers, she was as good as dead.

Chapter 11

If one more person asked her if she was all right, she was going to scream. Ray wasn't all right. She didn't think she could take one more thing going wrong. Didn't think that her life could get any more shitty. Ray thought that it very well could, but she didn't want it to. Too much too fast, was how it had been for her. Looking out the window at the children playing in the pool, she didn't even smile when what they were doing out there touched her heart. That part of her was hurting worst of all.

"Ray?" She told Denny that she didn't need anything. "I know, honey, but we should be heading out. Levi said that he'd meet you there after the funeral. He and his brothers are going to be the pall bearers for today. I'm going to be your shoulder to lean on if you need it."

"This should never have happened, Denny. Never." He said that he knew that. "What were they thinking, you suppose? Or were they? To allow something like this to happen when everything else is going fuck up."

"I'm so sorry, Ray. I really am." Nodding, she watched the kids as they played without any thought to the turmoil that was going on not ten feet away from them. "Come on, love. I'm to take you to the funeral home, and from there to the graveyard."

Ray didn't speak to anyone on their way in. It was too much effort to do that. But as soon as they pulled up in front of the funeral home, she sat there for several moments, just gathering her thoughts.

"She wasn't a nice person, was she?" Denny told her that if there were any that were more rotten, he never wanted to meet them. "Yes, well, you should have been living with her. Then you'd know."

"No thanks." He walked with her into the big room, and she was startled by how many flowers and arrangements there were. "I don't know this many people."

"You might not directly, but they sure know you. I'm thinking, too, that a few of them are from people that have worked with Levi. He knows of a few too." She nodded, and he caught her when she staggered a little. "Careful now, love. I don't know if I can push two wheelchairs at the same time. Your brother is here, but he can't stay long."

David was there? She moved to be with him, and smiled when he looked up at her. He'd been wounded badly when Caroline shot him. Then four days ago, Caroline had died from a massive heart attack that had killed her in her sleep.

"I didn't think you'd be coming. You're running late." She kissed David on the cheek and told him that she loved him. "I love you too. They said in a week, I'd probably get to come home. Are you ready for that?"

"Only if I can bundle you up in cotton and put you in a

safe place." He laughed, but was careful of it. "We'll have all your favorite meals. And birthday cake."

Ray had healed him. Not completely, she knew, but enough to stop the bleeding of his heart when the bullet entered it. She and Levi both had been able to remove the bullet by magic, and heal the large wound there to keep him from dying. Denny told her that it had been the only thing that had saved him, the removal of the bullet.

The service was to start in a few minutes, so she took the time to go to the casket. Caroline looked no different to her dead than she had when she was alive—mean and vengeful, her mouth pinched up like she had eaten a sour lemon. After making sure that she looked as good as they could get her, Ray wandered around the room looking at all the arrangements and the names of the people who had sent them.

There were so many of them, more than she would ever have to deal with. Since it was only her and David, who had a great many planters and such too, she had already decided to send them to the hospital. They'd have a card with them, telling the person that received them to have a lovely day. The funding that she'd set up was going to do a lot for the nursery, as well as the geriatric floor.

When she was told it was time, she sat in the front of the large room. A great many people had come today, mostly to make sure that Caroline was really dead, she supposed. Ray might well have done the same thing if she had heard that Ms. Spencer was deceased.

Going to the podium, Ray thought of all the things she could say about this woman. All the truths that would shock even the most worldly person. But today was for the living, not the dead woman beside her. Clearing her throat, Ray began.

"Several years ago, when I graduated from college, I thought that my life was perfect. Boy, did I have that wrong." A few people laughed. "My family is all gone now except for me and my brother. Am I sad? A little. But I've figured out since that day that things have a way of working their way around so that you have up and downs. I'm hoping, with the Stantons by my side, that I can move forward and have a few more ups than downs. Both David and I are."

Ray didn't talk about her aunt to the group—her grandmother, really. Nor did she talk about her father. They were both dead now, and there was no point in bringing up things that weren't worth it anymore. She did talk about her grandma, the woman that she missed more and more every day. And she spoke of the flowers that were around the room, and her plans for them.

"I'm going to start this with Caroline's things. I think she would have liked that a little." No one laughed, for which she supposed she was grateful. "She was a stern woman, my aunt, and she's gone to a better place."

When they moved out to the graveyard, she thanked people for coming. Interment was going to be next to her father's grave. The marker that she'd gotten for her father only mentioned that he was a father and son. Caroline's marker only said beloved daughter. Ray couldn't stomach putting anything about her being anything else.

There was going to be a reception at their home for anyone that wanted to come by. Lucy had put out a large basket, and put a little sign on it that said it was for donations to the nursery. It wouldn't have occurred to Ray to do something like that, but she knew that most of the people coming to the house were friends of the family. Levi never left her side after they took David back to the hospital to recover more.

"Mrs. Stanton, if you don't mind, I'd like to have a word with you. Your brother too, but I'm to understand that he is yet a minor, and cannot make any decisions." Ray asked the man, who she vaguely recognized, who he was. "Pardon me. I'm Paul Jenkins. I worked for a time for your aunt. And after her death, I called in a few favors, and we worked round the clock to get her estate settled for you."

"Mr. Jenkins, I don't know if you knew what sort of person my aunt was, but I want nothing to do with anything she might have left behind." He told her that he'd not thought she would. "Then why bother me about it?"

"As I said, a couple of other attorneys and myself worked hard to get it settled up for you, mostly to name you and David as the sole heirs to her estate. And in doing so, I have had a long conversation with your brother-in-law Christian. He helped us a great deal in setting things up for you to use the money." She told him that she didn't understand, and wasn't surprised to see Christian come stand with her and Levi. "We'll explain now if you don't mind letting us use your office."

After showing the men where it was, she said goodbye to a few guests. Once they were gone, she spoke to Barnes and had him bring in drinks. She was suddenly as dry as a desert. Going into her large office, she sat behind the desk with Levi.

"Ms. Spencer wouldn't have left you anything had she had her way about it. But in leaving it to her son, your father, she did you a great service—at least the foundations that you have taken upon yourself to open. Both the Geriatric Foundation and the Babies Basket Foundation will benefit greatly, if you would allow it." Ray looked over at Christian. "He said this would be the only way you'd want anything to do with the money."

"More than likely. What stipulations are on the money?" Mr. Jenkins told her that there were none. "You mean that I could use the money to hire a bunch of strippers, and that would be fine with you?"

"All right, yes, there are stipulations. The money is going to be divided in half, and the estate will be put in the two different accounts, to pay for whatever you need to benefit the causes. If I were you, when young David turns eighteen, I'd put him in charge of these. He has a good head on his shoulders, and was a great deal of help with telling us what you were doing with your own money."

"I don't mean to be impolite, Mr. Jenkins, but I didn't think my...that Caroline had all that much money. She spoke of it like she had billions, but I never actually saw her spend a penny. Not in all the time I knew her." He said that was right. "What do you mean, that's right? She didn't have any money?"

"No, I'm sorry. Ms. Spencer had billions. She was good at keeping it hidden away from the IRS and anyone else that might come snooping around. I'm not sure how she did it, but I can only figure that she threatened them in some way. And as you are well aware, she didn't spend it much. As far as I know, she never paid for anything at all but her utilities, and perhaps a repair on the house when it was necessary." Ray asked how many billions. "Thirty, Mrs. Stanton. And the money, if you'll allow it, will go for something kind, something needed, like your foundations."

"She'd hate that with every fiber of her being—you know

that, don't you?" Mr. Jenkins said that was a bonus as far as he was concerned. Ray laughed. It was the first one she'd had or felt like having since this all began. "I'd have to talk to David about it. He might want to use it for evil or something."

"He only wants enough to buy himself a car, which after the sale of the house — I'm assuming that neither of you wish to own that?" Ray told him no. "Then after the sale of the house and the contents, he'll have more than enough to do that, not counting the billions. Both of you will."

"What, if you know, did my father owe? And again, I'm only assuming that my father didn't have a pot to piss in." Mr. Jenkins said that all he had was his home, which was on the market now. "Caroline was going to sell that."

"Yes. When he passed away, everything he had went to his sister. In this circumstance, as he didn't know her real relationship to him, we didn't have to work around that. But she put his house on the market the day she found out he had died. Someone has gone through the house on her behalf and taken anything out that she wanted, which is still in a box in Ms. Spencer's house. That will be sold off, and the money from that will come to you as well."

"No, I most assuredly do not what anything from his estate." He asked if he could put it with Ms. Spencer's. "No. I'll find something to do with it. Perhaps give it to someplace that helps abused children. He'd hate that too."

"Very good." Mr. Jenkins handed her an envelope. "There are other properties that belonged to Ms. Spencer. Nothing that has any attachment to the rest of the estate, but were owned by her. Mostly I would call them slum homes — places that she collected rent from and did very little to nothing in trying to keep the people living there safe. Maybe you can have the Stantons advise you on those, and see if you can get better living places for the people living there."

She said that she'd take care of them. Nodding once, he headed for the door. When he turned back to her, she could see his smile, and thought that it was an odd one until he spoke.

"There were times when I wanted to kill Ms. Spencer myself. I'll not lie to you. She wasn't a nice person, as you said earlier, but I think she was the devil, or at least a spawn of him. If you should need help with the foundations that you've set up, I'd find it a great honor to help you. I'd work for free, as I have more than enough money for myself nowadays. It would be the only company that I'd help out, now that I've retired."

"I'll think about it, Mr. Jenkins. This is a great amount to throw at someone all at once." He said that he could understand that as well. "I do want to thank you for doing this for David and I. I would have simply not taken the money without thinking it through. You've made it better for everyone."

After he left them, the other people started to leave as well. In the morning, a courier service was going to pick up the flowers from the funeral home and take them to the ladies' club to be resorted and have cards put on them. The planters would be given to the families, so that they could get good homes as well.

Talking to David that night, she asked him what he'd think about working with her on this, and he was all for it. But he did want to finish college too. Ray told him that they could easily work around that.

~*~

152

Levi covered the paintings that were to be left behind this showing. His mom had taken some of the smaller pieces to the house with her and hung them. Wyatt had selected two for his offices, and the rest of them were waiting on the next bunch to pick out theirs. It was nice having his family's support, and he thought that it made him feel like he was really working toward a goal with them at his side now.

"What time will all this arrive at the gallery?" He told Ken what he'd been told—noon tomorrow. "And you still want me there to make sure that things are correct this time?"

"Yes. The show was nearly over when I realized that one of my paintings was hanging upside down." They both laughed about it. Now it was funny—that night he'd been royally pissed off. "And the flyers, they're all finished and ready to go out too?"

"I sent them to the gallery two days ago. I got a call from them as soon as they were handed off to tell me that they had them. Also, I'm going to have a few more printed up for you. Your family said that they wanted a few of them for their own personal use." Levi nodded, debating on whether or not he should have sent the one called *Love* to the gallery. "If you call the gallery and tell them to send that large picture back, I'm to tell Ray. She said that she'd beat you senseless, and that you'd never be able to hold a paintbrush again."

"She's scary when she gets like that, isn't she?" They laughed again as he put the phone back in the cradle. "Where is my lovely wife? Do you have any idea?"

"She and Sandra and Dane—now there is a scary woman— they're out picking out baby furniture. Doc Denny said that everything is moving right along, and that the baby is doing well. I'm terrified of being a father, Levi. It'll be so tiny." He smiled and Ken flushed. "I know that it would have to be small where it's growing, but still, I've never held anything that tiny that will be depending on me. I held the twins the other day, and Ruby. Tess told me that our baby would be smaller than them."

"You're going to make a great father, Ken. And I promise you, you'll be able to hold her just fine."

He was still debating on the picture when his phone rang. Ken said that he had it, and Levi went back to work on the piece that he'd been finishing up since this morning.

Ken called him to the phone about ten minutes later, and he was confused when the other man looked upset. Just as he was picking up the receiver, he asked what was going on. Ken told him that he couldn't tell him. That he didn't want to tell him.

"Hello, this is Levi Stanton." The man was talking to someone else, and that was one of the worst things he could have done around him. Levi thought that when you called someone up, you should be ready to speak to them. So, like he always did, he hung up the phone. But he waited there, just to see if it was important enough for someone to call him back. When the phone rang, he picked it up and started speaking before the person on the other end of the line could.

"If you call me, speak to me. If you don't have time, then call back later. I'm a very busy man, and I don't have time to be made to hold while you finish up a conversation that I have no part in." He said that he'd said his name was Stark, of Stark's Galleries. "I don't care what your name is. Now, what is it you want?"

"It's about the paining called *Love*. I have a patron here that wants to purchase it." Levi asked him if he'd invited him to see it. "No, sir. He was here paying for other paintings that he purchased when it came in. It arrived before the others because of it being uncrated to make it safe. So since it didn't have a crate around it, I wanted to make sure that it hadn't been damaged. It wasn't. But Mr. Layman wants to purchase it. I wouldn't call you on something like this, what with the showing a week away, but he's very insistent. He doesn't know your name, just to make sure you know that too."

"I would hope not." Levi sat down in his office chair. "I was actually debating on asking for it back. I'm not sure that it's something that I wish to sell."

"I can tell him that if you wish. And I'm sorry about earlier. I had to toss him out of my office just to make this call. I've never seen anyone so excited for something like that before. And it is beautiful—I would say that it's your best work ever. But this is our first showing together, and I want it to be right." Levi wasn't sure what to do until Ray came into the room with him. "As I said, it wasn't crated, but I can send it back to you tomorrow if you wish it back."

Ray asked him for the phone. "Mr. Stark, my wife is here now, and she wishes to talk to you about the painting. Give me one moment to talk to her about it, then she will be on the phone. Just don't piss her off." The man was still babbling about never doing that when Levi pushed the hold button. "They want to buy it. I didn't even put a price on it. I'm still not sure I want to sell it."

"If you sell it, I'll do another one with you." That made his cock stretch in his pants. "Perhaps I'll paint you this time and have some fun."

Ray took the phone off hold, pushing the speaker button so he could hear too, and started talking about it being a one

155

of a kind piece that he really did want to keep, and that the buyer would have to make it worth their while to part with such a piece.

"All right, Mrs. Stanton. Let me call you back on that. But it would help me a great deal if you were to give me a starting point." She tossed him a number, and Levi nearly fell off the chair he was sitting in. Ten grand, that was a lot of money for a single work of art for anyone, Levi thought. "I can work with that. Thank you. I'll call you back momentarily."

When she put the phone down, Levi asked her if she was kidding about the price. She told him that she wasn't, and if the man didn't buy it, what were they out? To her it was worth every penny.

"Besides, to see the look on your face when I offered to do a second piece with you would be well worth it if someone paid that price, don't you think?" Levi pulled her down to his lap and kissed her. "I came here to ask you something, and Ken told me about the buyer. I have a shipment of wood coming in, one that I got too good of a deal on to have turned down. Sugar maple."

"You do know that doesn't mean a thing to me. If you want to store it, that I can help you with. But as to what sort of wood? I have no idea. To me, trees are trees." They both knew that his statement wasn't true, but he loved to tease her. "There was once a lumber barn just outside of town near Trinway. I was there the other day and had it all cleaned out for you, in the event that your building isn't going up so easily with all this rain. Anyway, you can put it all there."

Ray kissed him and told him thanks just as the phone was ringing. She picked it up and smiled when she spoke to Mr. Stark. Winking, Levi left her to her project while he stood in front of his latest work. He both loved it and hated it at the same time.

Picking up his thinner brush, he made some strokes across the dragon he was painting and stood back. That was all it needed. The red made the dragon seem to pop off the page, and he was happy with it.

Telling Ken that he was finished, he went to find Ray. She was still on the phone. He sat down and watched her. She was the most beautiful creature he'd ever seen, and he loved her more and more with every breath he took.

When she hung up the phone, he put her on his lap again, this time facing him. "We're going to have to do another painting, I'm afraid. Are you all right with that? I know that the last time was such a strain on you."

Levi smacked her on the ass. "It was. So I'm assuming that he paid the ungodly price for the painting." Ray shook her head. "I thought you said it was that or nothing when you spoke to Stark."

"Apparently another patron came in. Mr. Stark actually called him and told this other buyer that his client, you, was selling one painting early, and did he want in on it. I guess he did. Stark said that a bidding war ensued almost immediately." He asked her how much. "Levi, you told your mom once that the most you'd ever sold a painting for was just under ten grand, right?"

Levi asked her again how much they'd paid for the painting. She was dancing around the room now, and he was getting excited too. The painting had special meaning to him—both of them. But the money would go a long way in making him have good memories of it as well.

"You're driving me crazy. What sort of figure did you get

for the painting, Ray? Am I going to have to beat you to get the amount off of you?" She laughed and came back to sit on his lap. He didn't care if she only got a buck or two over the ten grand. He was thrilled to have her so happy again. "Tell me or I tickle you."

"One point seven million dollars." Levi asked if she was kidding. "Nope. One point seven for an original work of art by my favorite artist."

Levi must have passed out after that, because he didn't remember anything else but her dancing around the room. And he knew she was going to tell him it was a joke when he asked again. But damn, that was funny that she'd done that to him.

Chapter 12

Ray wanted to drag Levi by the ear and introduce him to people. He was lurking around the corner of each room, and would skitter away when someone saw him. She thought he was creeping people out. He was her.

"He's not good around people." She glanced at Lucy when she spoke, and asked her if he'd always been that way. "Oh yes. Since he was just a little boy. When the others would be out there talking someone's arm off, Levi would be hiding behind my skirt. He was forever getting all tangled up in my feet."

"Would it bother you if I made him come out and be a part of this? I mean, I might have to threaten him." Lucy told her good luck and walked away.

Ray went to find Levi. Enough, as they say, was enough. But she got side tracked when she saw their painting. It was beautifully hung. The sold sign on it didn't deter people from wanting it. She knew that the gallery wouldn't tell who had purchased it, nor for how much, but it was fun watching people wonder about it.

Ray found Levi standing in the shadows. Jerking him forward into the room where the painting was, she told him that if he didn't go out there, she was going to tell them how he'd painted it.

"You will not." She cocked her brow at him and tapped her foot. Ray had seen his mother do that, and for the most part, it worked. "Ray, what do you think will happen if you do that? People will want their money back. And you know as well as I do, they're going to want us to do another, and they'll want to watch."

"Then you'd better get out there and show yourself. These people pay big bucks in order to have one of your pieces. And I heard from Mr. Stark, Kian, that he raised the prices on all your paintings across the board and they're still selling well." Levi looked around, like he was trying to find a place to hide. Instead of letting him, she grabbed him by the hand and pulled him to the first painting that she came to. It was one of his smaller works, at three feet by six feet, and people were talking about it.

The woman standing there turned and looked at them both. "Isn't this magnificent? I love this kind of work. I spent a great deal of time in Japan and China, and this painting here is just as beautifully detailed as any of them I saw there. I so love this. What do you suppose her inspiration is?" Ray asked if she knew the artist was a woman. The lady laughed. "Sometimes I think it is, others I think it's a man. I just don't know. But I'd give all my fortune to speak to the person who has this much talent for a minute."

Ray just looked at Levi, and he growled low and put out his hand to the woman. "I'm Levi Stanton, and this is my work. I'm so very glad that you like it. So do I."

The woman squealed and hugged Levi. When he was able to break free—she did have him in her arms very tightly—he laughed when she did. The woman was crying and stumbling over her words as she tried to tell Levi what the painting meant to her.

"I can see them, you know. The tigers and the other animals. I mean, they look real. I'm not sure that they're not, to tell you the truth. I was there, in that area, and I was able to— You should see the other works I have. Nothing compares to this one in its beauty and colors. You have made— Oh my, I'm overwhelming you." Mrs. Waterson, she said her name was, hugged Levi again, this time not so passionately. "I'm so sorry about this. I had no idea that you were so handsome either. There I go again. My husband—he passed some years ago—he told me that I so often let my mouth get much too far ahead of my brain. I'm so sorry about that."

"It's all right. And I love this one too. I'm going to have an entire series of animals painted in the same way. I've decided that animals are too beautiful to clutter up with too much around them. The one I've been working on in my studio, it's of giraffes, with a single tree close by."

Mrs. Waterson was the first of many that he spoke to after that. Levi expounded on the kind of canvas he used. Talked about Ken, who was his lifesaver when it came to cleaning up after him. He held her hand throughout, telling them all that she was his rock, that without her, he wouldn't have been able to paint *Love*.

There were many questions about it as well. How did he get it painted with it being so large? Did he have to lay it down to cover all the canvas? And through it all, Levi only smiled. And that made the mystery all the more questionable for the patrons.

"Come with me."

He had her hand, dragging her through the gallery so she didn't know how she was not to go with him. As soon as they were in Kian's office, he stripped her dress off of her and ravaged her mouth.

They couldn't get enough of one another. Every part of skin that was exposed was explored, tasted, and kissed. Before Levi was completely naked, she was down on her knees in front of him, taking his thick cock into her mouth.

"Yes, baby. Make me come." She licked the side of his shaft. Fondled his balls until they were tight in her hand. And when Levi put his hand on her head, she could feel him touching the back of her throat with his cock, making her swallow him down until she was screaming around him with her release.

Levi was fucking her hard, his moans enough to make her come over and over. And when he dug his nails into her hair, she knew that he was coming, that he was going to make her come with it.

He exploded into her. Touching his balls with her palm, the heat from them was enough to make her moan again. That was all it took to have him coming again, to have him fucking her mouth all over and crying out her name.

She was so ready. Her body burned with the need to come too. She had, several times as a matter of fact. But they were not as satisfying as she knew that he'd give her. And when he picked her up, bending her over the desk in the room, Ray cried out when he slammed into her from behind, his teeth digging deeply into her shoulder as his other hand pressed against her clit so hard that she had to bite her own hand to stop from screaming loud enough to bring the building down around them.

When he bit her again, Ray felt his teeth touch bone. Felt the way that her muscles were torn. And when he came into her again, bringing her over the steep cliff that they were standing by, she closed her eyes from the quick movement of memories that weren't her own. The pain of the bite, the way he was abusing her body, were too much for her. And when she came again, this time there wasn't any holding back, she let the darkness take her under. As if she had a choice, she thought.

Levi was on the phone when she woke. Cradled in his arms, she curled into the heat of his body and realized that he had dressed. She was just getting up to look for something to wear that would make her feel as comfy as Levi looked. Ray cried out when she was suddenly dressed in the same manner, all the way to the fuzzy socks that he had on.

"I'll have to call you back. Can I reach you at this number that came up when you called?" The person must have said yes, because Levi answered like he had. "All right then. Give me about an hour and I'll see what I can find out for you."

"I'm dressed." Ray shook her head, and Levi nodded after putting his phone away. "No, you don't understand. I was thinking of comfy clothing, and this is what was just on me."

"I forgot to mention that. It's from Dane and her magic." She asked him if there was much more he'd forgotten to tell her. "Yes. I'm sure there is, but it's doubtful I can remember it all. That call was from a man by the name of Steward. Ever heard of him? He's a CO of the police department in

Middletown."

"No, should I have?" Levi shook his head and stood up. "Why did you think I might know him?"

"No reason. I was just trying to figure out which one of us he's trying to reach. He has no first name, you see, only a last. And you're a doctor, though not medically, the same as I am, so I was just trying to find out who. There was an explosion down there. School bus for privileged children. Killed three of the kids, and injured a dozen other kids and adults that were nearby waiting for another bus, a local school bus, to come by and get them." Ray asked him what that had to do with one of them. "The bus driver asked for him to find a Doctor Stanton. The CO is a cougar too, and thought of one of us first thing."

"You think that it's Wyatt's mate?" Levi said he didn't know. But the woman, the driver, was in critical condition and might not make it. "Then we have to gather all of us together that can go and see about her. Even if she's not his, there is a chance that one of us can help her."

"I have to talk to my family first. To see if anyone knows this man. Steward. I don't know why, but I believe it's going to be my dad who knows him. The man on the phone, he sounded older, about my parents' age. I don't know if he is or not, but that's what I'm going with right now." She asked where his dad was. "The gallery is still open. Not for much longer, but we should get dressed and go out there. You relaxed me enough so that I might be able to handle the rest of the night."

It was a good thing they could dress themselves, she thought later as they were leaving the expansive office. Her other dress was in shreds, her shoes had been broken at one point, and her hair had been a horrific mess. But other than the smile that was on their faces, she didn't think that anyone could tell what they'd been up to. Ray didn't want to think about what Levi said about them being able to smell it.

It was his dad that knew the man. They'd gone to college together, it seemed, and Levi gave him the phone number to call. Dane found her and Levi a few minutes later, while they were gathering up to leave, and told her what she knew about the explosion.

"Five kids were on the bus when it went up. The sixth kid had dropped his papers on the ground, and the driver, Bryn Dell, which I don't think is her real name, got off to help him pick them up." Levi said that was nice of her. "No, it wasn't. It's company policy for these drivers. They can't assume that someone isn't going to school because they're not out there waiting. They have to call the house, ask if he or she is going to class today, and then wait on them. Even that would get the driver into trouble if the kids arrived at the school late."

"Christ, you're kidding me." Dane handed her a picture of the crime scene. "Two of the kids survived this? How?"

"I don't know. Two things I don't know, but I'm going to find out. Why did she have to stop for someone to hand one of the kids something? And what was in it?" Levi asked her how she knew that much. "Cameras are on every bus, inside and out. A butler came running to the bus, but I can't tell if he had something in his hand when he got there. And Porsche Humphrey, one of the deceased, takes it from the butler, but you never see it again. She turns after getting it."

"You believe that is what caused the explosion." Dane told Levi that she didn't have enough to go on to tell what caused it. "You're going to assist?"

"Yes. So is the rest of the family. I insisted. If this woman is Wyatt's mate, we have to protect her at all costs. Even if she's not, then we still have to help her. I don't know, call it civic duty. But I need to know why she called Denny." Levi told her what he'd found out about the CO going to school with their dad. "Perhaps, but the girl asked for him. And begged the man to find Doctor Stanton."

Before they landed at the airport they had more information, but not enough to answer any questions any of them had. In fact, Ray thought there were more questions than answers. She was given the handbook to go over. Something that the woman said before she was able to get off the bus had bothered Steward. And he wanted to get to the bottom of it.

~*~

Denny read over the chart twice before he sat down next to the bed. Bryn had come through surgery all right, but she was far from out of the woods. In fact, he'd been surprised that they'd even tried to bring her back after she coded so many times.

Denny read the part where she had coded three times before they got her here, and once more on the operating table. The child was lucky to be alive. But he did wonder what her quality of life would be after this. Not to mention how happy she'd be with those that had tried to keep her here. He was sure that he'd not be. Not even as a cat would his kind have been able to make it this far, not with what had happened to her.

"You should have died as soon as the rod came out of the bus and made its way through you, the medic's told me. I cannot imagine what agony you were going through pulling those two children off the bus with that thing hanging out of you. Not to mention the second and third degree burns over most of your body." He wondered if the people whose children had perished in the fire would see her as the hero that he did. No, he knew, they would not. "My family is looking into this for you. We're going to get to the bottom of it, you can count on that. And when we do, you'll be all right. I hope so, anyway."

He watched the machine breathe for her. Her lungs were burnt too — dark suet had entered her, and was infecting her lungs as well as the rest of her. Bryn's large intestine had been damaged so badly that a part of it had to be removed. Her bowel was going to have to be taken care of soon too. The surgery was only to save her life. She would have to get better before they could fix anything that might have been broken. And that wasn't even including the bones that had been broken or shattered. Broken, he thought, as in she'd never be able to use them again without constant pain.

"I contacted your father, like I was supposed to. I'm assuming that is why you contacted me. And your sister too. I couldn't find Walker, but I'm sure that Addi knows where he is." They had been a close family a long time ago, and the years and bad news had torn them apart. Mostly because of their mother, but each of them had their reasons for scattering to the winds and changing their names. "Addi isn't coming here yet, as you can guess. When she finds your brother, she will tell him the same. To wait until I call them again."

He couldn't say aloud that they were waiting to see if she died or not — whether one of them would have to come here and claim her body. It was a gruesome ordeal, he thought, to have to come to a different state and claim the body of one so young and so battered.

Denny thought about their father. A good man by all

accounts when he'd known him—someone that could be trusted. If he called you friend, which many he did not, Leslie would have your back, front, and any other part of you that needed protecting.

And most of that was still true. Leslie had money, a great deal of it. But most thought that he'd gotten it the easy way—by selling drugs, dealing with prostitution, as well as murder and robbery. But, like Denny, he was good with money and had invested it wisely. That was the reason that his kids had taken off. They had believed every rumor around. And, honestly, Les hadn't ever been a demonstrative man. He'd given them money, and had continued to help them—behind the scenes, so to speak. Leslie was saving them—from himself.

Now, Denny knew that since Leslie's children had gone and weren't able to talk to him, just be with him, he'd fallen apart. His businesses were still doing well. Leslie had a string of houses that he used to visit with his children that were being sold off one at a time. And the house that had once held the happiest people he knew was in disarray, the yards unkept. The man that lived there had become a hermit—and he looked like one too.

The last time that he'd gone to see him, Denny had begged him to go home with him. But he was stern in his reasoning. He was afraid that people would think the same of him. Denny had a reputation to uphold. Leslie's, he told him, was gone forever. It was the saddest thing he'd ever witnessed, a man down on his luck, who still had the world at his fingertips.

"I didn't try to reach Kitty. The last time I spoke to your father, he told me that she was in a bad way. I took her money from him, but I couldn't get her to take it. She believes, as others do, that your father is the worst kind of scum." And he wouldn't say it out loud, but that was Meadow's fault—the kids' mother. "Meadow is married again, in case you didn't know. She didn't have any more children of her own, but there are one or two that her new husband had. I'm keeping an eye on things for Leslie. And now you too."

Denny tried to think of something that would be a good story. He knew that someplace in his head was one—a trip that Bryn's family had taken. Leslie used to call him up, telling him about the places that they'd visited, and always had a story about something that had befallen them. Usually it was silly things, but a few had been close calls.

"Remember the trip you all took to that amusement park? You must have been about thirteen then. Your dad was so proud of you all, but you most of all. Leslie said that without blinking an eye, you and your sisters and brother gathered up water from the vendors, using your own money to buy it, and handed it out to people that looked like they needed it. It was too hot, he told me, for a lot of those people to be out in the sun. But you guys, you saw a need and took care of it. I think he nearly busted buttons off his shirt that day telling me about it."

There were other stories too. They'd been driving along, and even though they were all stuffed in the car, Bryn had asked to pick up the hitchhiker on the way home from the movies. The man had been headed home—his mom was passing, and that was the only way he could get to her. Bryn asked for enough money to pay for his plane ticket, promising her dad that she'd pay him back, and sent the man on his way.

"Then a week later, after your dad thought that you'd been duped, there was a card for you, and a picture of the man and

169

an elderly lady in the hospital." He thought of Leslie, who had been paid back by his youngest daughter. "The clipping was from the newspaper, telling how he'd made it home for his mother's passing, and that she had died that evening with a smile on her face. The obit even thanked the strangers who had made it possible for him to be with her in her hour of need. The man had mentioned in the card to you that he'd not tell your names, because he didn't want people everywhere coming for a handout."

"Dad?" He turned and looked at Wyatt. "I was wondering if you're finished with her chart. And before you ask me too, I don't know if she's my mate. The smells in here are too strong, and all I can focus on is how badly she's been hurt."

"Yes, I'm finished." He handed him the chart and turned back to Bryn. "She has family that is coming in—her father for now, I hope. I've made arrangements with Dane to make sure that her father is safe. If he'll make the trip."

"Bad blood between them?" He told him what had happened, the watered down version of it anyway. "I see. And her siblings? Are they coming in too?"

"No, I don't think so. They've drifted apart over the years. I bet it's been ten years since any of them have spoken to their father. Talking to each other would have been just as bad, I'm sure that Leslie would have thought. It's funny, really—the man never did a terrible thing in his life, yet he's been tried and convicted without even having a trial." Wyatt asked him what had happened. "Well, it's been weighing heavily on my mind since we got the call, how this all began. Leslie was good at guessing how things would turn out, like he had some sort of inside track on things. He did win more than his fair share of lottery money—never the big stuff, not at first. But he was good at the ponies as well. Made his first million dollars by hitting it good at the tracks."

"I'm making a mental note to myself not to play cards with him if I ever get to meet him." Denny laughed and told him that was a good idea. "I'm sure that he was investigated on the winnings, right? I mean, if he was that good, people would have questioned him."

"Yes. Everyone did for a time. And Leslie, being a good man, didn't think a thing about it." Denny looked at the young woman in the bed beside him. "Then Walker got into trouble. Nothing big, just trouble that any kid would get into—he fathered a child at sixteen. The family, they wanted him dead, and Leslie thought to give them money. And that was when it all began to go downhill for them. Meadow, his wife at the time, wasn't helping matters by talking to the press, lying to them about what an abusive person Leslie was. Other things too. And with people already questioning him about his luck, it was like a flame had been flared up, and he was being accused of a great many things."

He talked to his youngest son about the things that Leslie would do with his family—art museums, amusement parks, and long vacations. Wyatt said it was much like their childhood, going places as a family instead of being left at home so that he and Mom could go alone.

"We had you boys and you were our responsibility. The thought of not sharing one of our adventures with you six was just sad to me. I think that Leslie felt the same way. For a time, anyway." Denny watched the nurse come in and take readings on the many monitors that Bryn was on.

"Her prognosis isn't good, is it, Dad?" He shook his head, saddened by the fact that someone so young was going to be taken from this world. "What would happen, you think, if Dane were to come and help her along?"

"I already asked her. She didn't think that Bryn would appreciate us keeping her alive with so many things hurting her. She's going to lose her leg, and most of the fingers on her left hand are gone. Bryn's left eye is gone too — the fire had done a good deal of damage to it, I'm afraid. And she'll be eating her meals from a tube if I don't miss my bet."

The monitors started to scream at them, and they were pushed out of the way.

Almost as soon as they came in with the crash cart, everything settled down. The monitors no longer screamed, but beep-beeped at her ever-slowing heartrate. Yes, Denny thought sadly, this child wasn't long for this world. And if her dad was going to get to see her, he'd better get his ass in gear. The poor thing wasn't going to make it until morning, Denny realized.

Going into the hallway when they were changing her dressings, he pulled out his phone. It was time to make that difficult call — to gather the Mackenzie's together for the death of their sister.

Chapter 13

Levi was having fun. The street fair had brought out everyone to see what was being sold, or even just to look at things. He was painting faces, of all things, and enjoying it more than he had most other things he'd done. Children and adults alike were standing in line to have him put a butterfly on their faces, or one of the many other things that he'd decided to paint today. Standing up after painting the little girl's face from down the street, he looked over at his family.

Colton was handing out flyers and other things that he'd picked up about suicide prevention. He was also writing a book about it. The little paper fans he had to give away were perfect for the warm weather, and they had the number that a person could call for help right on it.

Dad and Mom were walking around, sampling jellies and jams. A man was selling bread, and Dad was carrying a couple of loaves of it. Mom had a pink bag in her hand that Levi knew had fudge in it. Mom had a real sweet tooth when it came to chocolate fudge.

In the morning, he knew they were headed back to the hospital. Bryn was still holding on—waiting, Dad told him, for her dad. He didn't think he was wrong about that.

Brayden had asked the men working on a project for the library in town to save up all the pieces of wood. Then he and Dane had sanded them off and had painted them bright colors. Everyone that came by their booth had to try their hand at building a tower, and the adult with the tallest one at the end of the fair would get a hundred-dollar gift card. The child with the tallest would get all the blocks. There had to be a couple of hundred of them, too.

Christian was helping Allie show some defensive moves. He was mostly getting beat to shit, but Levi thought he was having fun too. Allie's laughter could be heard all over town, she was having so much fun. And her dad, who had opened the gym for handicapped veterans, was handing out flyers for that as well.

Jules, as mayor, was busy being mayor, and showing off his triplets. They were only a set of twins they'd adopted and Tess's baby girl, but you'd not be able to tell from the way that Jules talked about them. Levi had overheard someone telling his wife that he'd never seen a daddy so proud of a child pooping its diaper before.

Wyatt was running the first aid booth, but mostly he was fending off single and married women. The little girls too, each of them, had a major crush on his brother. Wyatt was the type of guy that women could depend on when they needed muscles, and also the first person they'd call when they needed a shoulder to cry on. He said it was both a burden and a joy to be himself.

Levi painted the next person's face and made him look

like Batman. The kid had a shirt on that was covered in the masked man, but the child had been thrilled to death that Levi had painted him just right. The girl standing next to the boy just rolled her eyes at her brother, calling him a moron. The girl sat in his chair next.

Reaching out to Hailey, he asked her what the child's fondest dream was. He thought that she'd want to be a faerie princess, a prom queen, or something along those lines. But no, he was as surprised as Hailey was when she thought about being someone to save the fishes in the oceans. Levi started painting all the ones that Hailey sent him images of that were in the child's head. He spoke to her, as he did every person that sat down.

"The first time I decided that I wanted to be an artist, we were at the zoo. We saw all the animals that day. My mom had made us a picnic dinner that we set up under the trees in the little park." She said that they had gone to the zoo too. "After we were all finished, we were about set to go home. My little brother was tired, and my dad had a headache. He said it was all the smells, but I think we were driving him crazy a little, dragging him and Mom all over the place." Sally, her name was, giggled. "Yes, there were six of us at the zoo that day, not counting my parents. Anyway, there was time to see one more exhibit before we had to leave. I think it was Brayden that wanted to go to the aquarium. He wanted to see how they constructed the pools. I didn't care where we went so long as there was a drink at the end. I was very thirsty."

"When we were there, a woman let us touch all the fish. I wasn't afraid at all. I got to touch a star fish and a shark. It was the best there was. The next time we went, I wanted spend all my time there. But we'd have to pace ourselves, my dad said.

It was too expensive to go every day like I asked if we could." After she spoke, Levi, who had planned to paint a starfish on her face, decided on a shark. Painting it while everyone stood watching, he listened to her as well as she had listened to him. "My brother Parker, he hates fish when we have it for dinner. But this was so different. They were so beautiful and soft. I know that there are a lot of dangerous ones in the ocean, but I loved every second of it. Did you paint one when you got home, Mr. Levi?"

"The manatee. All the others too, but the manatee seemed to call out to me to paint. So when I did, my mom took a picture of it and sent it to the man in charge of the zoo. They asked to buy it, so that they could auction it off for donations for more animals and to keep the others fed." He was finished with her face, but she wasn't finished listening to him. "I wanted to help the fish too, you see, so I told them that they could have the picture. You know what they did? They gave me a pass to get into the zoo whenever we wanted. Wasn't that really nice of them? Here you go, Sally, tell me what you think."

While she admired her face in the big mirror, Levi pulled out his wallet. Handing the pass to Sally's father, he told him that it was still good and that the zoo had told him that he could pass it on. He wanted his family to have as much fun as they wanted, and to go as often as they wanted, as he and his family had.

"How much did you pay for the painting to buy it back, Mr. Levi?" He laughed, and told him. "And did you donate it a second time? I'm betting you did."

"Yes. Three times. But my mom, who was buying it from them, told me that was enough. She would own the zoo if I kept that up." They were both laughing as they walked away.

And Levi felt wonderful.

While he was painting the next child, Hailey contacted him again.

That was nice of you, Levi. I'm going to hire the man, by the way. He asked if they were on hard times. *The hardest. He put in his application for the new plant that's being finished up. I wasn't going to hire him when he told me that he'd not be able to start working until after Monday. That was the day that they'd planned to take their children to the zoo. One last fling in the event that neither of them got a job soon. I didn't know that at the time, but I do now. He should have told me. I would have bent over backwards to make sure that he had a job. But you had to go and show me up, didn't you?*

Yes, and I love you too, Hailey.

Dane came by to bring him a bottle of water and a sandwich later. He ate it while she painted some faces. Taking his hour break, they walked along the booths, buying things that they didn't need and eating more than they should have. He'd weigh a ton if this kind of thing went on yearly, but it was also a blast.

Howard Hamby had had only a month to throw this thing together, and he'd done a fine job of it. Levi wondered what he'd do with an entire year to plan the next event. Howard had also been put in charge of the rest of the events of the year, including the Christmas lighting ceremony that had been held every Christmas Eve since he'd been a little boy.

The fair closed up at five, and they were all meeting back in town at six-thirty. Everyone was bringing a covered dish, and his family was supplying and cooking all the burgers and hot dogs. They were having ham and chicken salad too, and Levi couldn't wait to sit down and eat.

177

Showing up early to help put the tables and chairs out, he was surprised to see how many people were already there. And how many extra tables and chairs were being brought in from the high school to accommodate them. It wasn't at all hard to see that everyone had enjoyed the day, and were now ready to sit down and have dinner.

He snagged a plate of food for him and his brothers to munch on while they cooked and the women of the family were handing out bottled drinks. There were napkins, which he never would have thought of, being handed out by the older kids in the family.

At ten the townspeople helped to clean up. Then everyone gathered up blankets and chairs to go out to the Stanton ranch to watch the fireworks. He was glad now that he'd used some of his money to pay for them for today. As far as he was concerned, it was the perfect way to end a perfect day.

Walking back to their house with her hand in his, Ray told him that she'd overheard someone asking Howard if he was going to do this at the Fourth of July picnic. Levi laughed, and said that he'd have to sell some more pictures to do that again.

"It was well worth it. And I'm sure if you asked, any one or all of your brothers would have helped." He nodded. "Levi, what if when Wyatt finds his mate, you and I go on a nice long vacation? I was thinking a cruise, but I wasn't sure about that, what with you being a scaredy cat and all."

Levi chased her all the way home. Ray would get a little ahead of him and he'd have to race to catch up. Levi couldn't wait to take her on this cruise. He had booked it a few days ago when Hailey came and told him what Ray had been thinking about. It was his pleasure and his duty to make his little wife happy, Levi thought.

~*~

Ray was busy working on the next design when she realized that she was alone in the big building. It didn't occur to her to keep track of the time. She'd been so deep into studying the way the chairs fit under the table that she'd tuned everything out.

The computers were all off and the phones were no longer ringing off the hook. Afraid for a moment, she reached out to Lucy to see what she'd missed. Ray knew that Levi was painting, and she didn't want to bother him with something silly.

"Missing? Nothing that I know of, other than it's nearly seven in the evening. Do you have an alarm on your phone, Ray? I'm thinking that you either need an assistant like Ken to keep you in food, or you need to set alarms." She asked if she'd spoken to Levi. "Yes, he came here, as he didn't want to disturb your creative juices. My goodness, two artists in one family is going to be the death of me. Come here, child. I'll have something to eat for you when you arrive."

Walking to the other home, she marveled at all the color that was everywhere now. Not only the plants that had been planted in the planters along Main Street, but there was plenty of green in the woods with bits of color. Ray often wondered if it did this in the spring, sprouted all the amazing colors so that you'd feel better about the weather that had just left.

Ray smiled when she saw Denny. However, that turned into a frown when she saw how exhausted he looked. He'd been at the hospital every day for the last few days. He said that he was keeping young Bryn company until her dad arrived. Ray didn't think the other man was going to come, and that broke her heart too.

"How is my lovely artist today?"

She told him she thought she was better than he was, and that apparently was all it took for the man to break down. He held onto her, sobbing about how much he hated that the child was suffering. That he didn't know what else to do to help her, and that he was sure, as she'd been only moments ago, that Bryn's father wasn't going to come and see his child once before she died.

"I'm so sorry, Denny. I truly am." Denny held her tightly, still crying, but not like he had been. "If I had his phone number, I'd call him up right now and explain to him the meaning of love. Because for all his procrastinating, he's going to miss the one thing that should make him want to come from the hells of earth — the death of one of his children. But here you are, a man with a family that would do anything in the world for him, taking care that she's not alone. You know what? He just is a mean old turd, and he's sitting there on his fat ass and not doing a damned thing. Just give me his number."

Ray stood there with her hand out, tapping her foot. Denny looked her up and down, and then started laughing — and hard, too. Ray was sure that she'd overstepped her boundaries, or she'd insulted his friend. While she was trying to think what she'd said, Denny finally started talking.

"You are a deadly combination of my wife, who I love dearly, and Dane right now. Scary potty mouth and tapping foot, to make a point." Denny hugged her. "You've made this old man feel good right now. Better than I have in days. Yes, you know what, I think I will give you his number. Let you tell him just what you think of him being too afraid to come out of hiding for Bryn."

"I will, you know. You give me that number, Denny, and he's going to get a piece of my mind. My fist too, if I can figure out how to shove it at him through the phone." He pulled out the tattered paper with the man's name and phone number on it. "He's going to regret messing with my family."

Stomping into the house, Denny was right behind her. But almost as soon as she smelled the bacon cooking, she was starving. Begging for something to eat while she laid out her plan to talk to Mr. Mackenzie, Ray had it all worked out before she picked up the phone.

"My name is Rachel Stanton. I need to— Excuse me? What did you say to me?" She was waiting on the man to stop stammering. When he didn't, she spoke again. "Look, buster. I've had it about up to my ears with this bullshit. You put that man on this phone right fucking now, or I'll come there and show him what a loving father does with a dying child. Dr. Denny is the best there is, and has been sitting with that man's child now since she was brought in. You put that man on the phone, or expect me to come there. And buddy, you so don't want that to happen."

"Mrs. Stanton, I'm Leslie MacKenzie. My butler handed me the phone right about the time you said you were tired of the bullshit. I assure you, I am as well. Not from you. But I had to make sure that my daughter was really there before I could travel. I'm not in a good place myself. I'm leaving today for your lovely town. I shall be there in a couple of hours." She said she was sorry. "No, don't be. I'm glad to know that my daughter is being cared for. And tell Denny that I'll talk with him as soon as I get there. Tell him thank you. From one father to another, thank you."

Ray told Denny and the rest of them what he'd asked

her to tell him. She felt foolish now, like she'd trampled over someone's flowers and messed them all up. Denny started laughing when she told him how she felt.

·"Don't feel that way. He's more than likely laughing about it right now. Les is a good man, one that you'll find out is very paranoid over things that aren't out there. He has believed since his wife left him that he's a wanted man, when I have assured him, as have people that would be in the know, that he is not." He laughed again. "You sure did get him going. I'm betting right now that he's not only having everyone speed up their getting him on that plane, but he's moving too. That man is a bigger procrastinator than anyone I've met. But he is also one of the best men I've ever had the pleasure of being friends with."

"Why has he kept out of his children's life? I mean, if he really isn't wanted or whatever he thinks is going on, why has he not tried to contact or be with his kids?" Denny said that he honestly didn't know. "Did you know that Bryn was only a few days from getting her PhD? That she was planning to work for the government as a translator? In order to do this, she had to sleep in her car a few times when books were more than she anticipated. School was always before anything else in her life."

"I didn't know that, no. I would have been there for her, as she well knows. But why he's doing this? I haven't any idea, Ray."

He asked her if Dane had looked into it. "No, I don't think so. She's been working on another project that is taking up a great deal of her time. I didn't want to bother her."

"She might be just the one to convince him." He stood up, and she waited while he spoke. "When he arrives, you should know that he'll have a group of men with him. All of them will be trained to kill before asking questions. I have it on good authority that he rarely if ever goes anywhere without them."

"So expect a militia group of people. I'll talk to Dane. Perhaps we can out gun his men and have them behave." Denny laughed as he left her in the kitchen.

Ray decided to go to the studio and see how Levi was doing. She was too tired to work today anymore.

"Levi? Can I come in?" He was covered in paint when he opened the door. It was even in his hair. Also, she thought that he looked a little manic. "Levi?"

He grabbed her hand and dragged her across the room. There was a canvas set up, but she could only see the back of it. Levi turned to her and then looked at the canvas before he started talking.

"I came out here last night to just work on the canvas. Ken can do it, but I like to get involved with something else when a painting starts to form in my head. And after just doing this one canvas, I had to stop and get out the paints. I was so glad when Ken had—" She put her hand over his mouth, and she could feel his smile forming. Removing her hand, he kissed it and spoke more calmly. "I need you to strip and lay down on the table for me."

"Sure you do." He nodded, and looked so serious that she started unbuttoning her blouse. "If you wanted me naked, you could have started with that."

"I need to finish this up, and you're going to be my main focus in this. A hidden gem. That's the name of it, by the way. Hidden Gem. Hurry, Muse is being very impatient with you." When she was naked, he had her lie on the table that held

183

other paints. "Okay, I'm going to arrange you, but I need you to just trust me on this."

"I have, and will always, trust you." With a quick kiss on her mouth, he started putting paint containers around her. Mostly it was in front of her breasts and her nether region, but he was painting small works on her too. "Levi, is this a painting that I'm going to be embarrassed about?"

"No. Trust me."

When he seemed satisfied with what he'd done, he stepped back. It took him three more times before he seemed happy with what he was doing. Then he draped a dark green piece of silk over her feet.

Going back to the canvas, he began painting. He was putting strokes here and there, looking at her, then going back to work. Ray didn't enjoy having someone talk to her when she was working, so was comfortable with the silence while he worked.

When he stepped back to look at the canvas, he looked at her again. There was more paint on his face, where he had rubbed his cheek at some point. And his hair was sticking straight up with a dap of yellow.

After he arranged more colors around her, she noticed that, like her, he would zone out. She'd bet that she could have a conversation with him and he'd never hear her. As she laid there, not at all feeling uncomfortable, she thought of the design she was doing and how it was giving her fits.

The table was going to be one that would collapse onto itself. There would be a crank or electrical function that would raise one or two leaves, depending on the need, into place so that it could be enlarged. The chairs that would be able to accommodate the larger size would fit up under the table.

Out of the way, she wanted them.

She had the design worked out — it was getting the chairs out without much in the way of effort that was the problem. The fact that they fit perfectly under the table and looked like extra legs was a design that she'd used before, but it hadn't sold well because of the simple fact that the chairs were too difficult to remove.

Once the chairs were out, a person could pull the back up from the seat and lock it in place with a simple slide lock. They weren't as wide as the other four chairs, but they would hold a good sized person. Just as the problem was going to have to be put on the back burner, she felt one of the others — Brayden, she thought — speak to her.

I can help you with that. She asked him if he was reading her mind. *No. I didn't have to. You're projecting the problem so loudly that, as the leap leader, I could feel your frustrations. But, as I said, I can help you with the chair issue. Tell me what you've tried so far.*

I've tried everything I know to make it work. It's getting them to pull out by a single person that is the issue. They're not heavy nor are they bulky, but they just won't come out without lifting the table up and pulling them from under it. He asked if she'd tried making the legs just an inch shorter. *Yes. And all that did was make it more difficult to pull them out because they were still stuck up under the table.*

What if, like the table, they had a crank on them that pushed all four of them — I'm assuming that's what you have. She said that it was. *All right. So you have this crank in the table that when used, it not only pushes the leaves up, but the chairs out at the same time. It would be easy enough to design. I could even show you how to do it.*

I didn't think of that. But wouldn't it scratch up the floor they were on if they were scraped along the floor like that? He told her that was when she'd make them just a small inch shorter than the table legs that were stationary. *Oh Brayden, I think that might work. But I'd like for them to be like the crank I have already. That they can be moved electrically too. I do sell a lot of my designs to the handicapped, and I need it to be easy for them as well.*

No problem. I can work on that today. I'm sort of bored, what with Dane out of town. And then when I have it ready, you can work it into your table, and there you go. She asked him if he'd mind if she put his name on the design. *No, I wouldn't mind, but that's not necessary. I just love this sort of thing. It's my passion, you might say.*

"Ray?" She looked at Levi when he said her name. "I'm finished. Are you all right? You look like you've solved the world's greatest problem."

"I have for me. Can I see it now?" He nodded, and looked a little embarrassed. She pulled on the shirt that he handed her and walked to the canvas. "Oh Levi. It's stunning."

Chapter 14

Les sat next to his little girl. He couldn't touch her — they'd told him that she was so sensitive to everything that he had to be careful not to even speak loudly. So he pulled out his notes that he'd made on the plane that he wanted to talk to her about, and looked at the face that had been so very dear to him all her life.

"I messed up, my love. I should have been here for you, for all of you. Now I don't know my children at all." He looked down at his notes, blurred now because he was crying again. "I heard what you did for those children. I'm so very proud of you. The police told me that you wouldn't even leave when you knew that they were dead, and wanted them off the bus before you were."

He thought of the other things that Bryn had said to them. That she would have been fired had that happened. Les was having someone look into those rules, and the place that she had worked for.

The second thing on his list was a little harder for him to

talk about.

"I'm to understand that instead of asking for help from me, you had to sleep in your car. I cannot tell you, my dear, how profoundly sorry I am about that. In my mind you were safer to not have anything to do with me, but I've been told I wasn't correct." He thought of the way Dane and the other women had torn into his ass when he'd landed. "You should have heard them, Bryn. I'm sure you would have been cheering them on. And my men I brought with me, they didn't move, not even to draw their guns. You want to know why? The men she brought were bigger, and their guns were at the backs of my men's heads. Quite the coup, if you ask me." He nodded, and thought of the way he'd been proven wrong after all these years. "I've talked to Walker and your sisters. As you can well imagine, it took some powerful apologizing too. Something I will do for the rest of my life."

The nurse came in and checked the fluids that were being put into his baby girl. He asked her if she was doing all right, and she only had to shake her head. It was then that he realized that they'd only been keeping her alive for him. When she left him, Les sobbed like he'd never done before. Bryn wasn't going to make it.

"I'm so sorry, baby. I'm so very sorry." He cried until he thought there was nothing left in him. Touching his finger to her own, he marveled at how brave she'd been, and he had only to reach out and he could have been with her forever. With all of them. "I'm a horrible man. And the worst father in the world. Why you wanted me here, I will never know. Nor will I ever forgive myself for not keeping you in my life and my heart."

Les knew that his other children had struggled. Most of

them, at some point, had less money and security than Bryn had when going to college. Addi had been hurt the most by his actions of pushing them away. For some reason, he most wanted her, of all his children, to forgive him. And he knew that putting money into all their bank accounts was never going to make up for the issues, the problems that he'd caused them by being nothing but a recluse. A bastard recluse.

"They're coming too, Bryn. I know that you're only here because you wanted me to be. And I have no words to tell you once again that I'm sorry. I keep saying that, and know that it's too little too late, but I'm going to make it up to you. Somehow, I'm going to do something that will get me through the gates of heaven so that I can see you once again."

The monitors started beeping, and he waited while they checked on her. Before the people could get into the room, the sounds stopped. Her heartrate, he could see, was slowing again, and he knew that it wasn't going to be long now.

"I've spoken to your mother — or I had someone speak to her. She's unable to come here. Her life, I'm told, is something of a mess." It was a lie — he knew that even Bryn would know that he'd lied. Meadow didn't want anything to do with the children, any more than she wanted to be around him. "She might come later. I don't know. It's difficult to get anything nailed down right now."

Walker, his son, was getting dressed when he looked out the window of the room she was in. The burn unit, where she was, didn't allow anyone to come in that wasn't dressed in a way to keep out germs. At this point he was sure that it didn't matter, but the hope made him want to do whatever was needed. Walking into the little dressing room that Walker was in, Les couldn't believe that this was his son. His first

189

born. He'd turned into a man at some point.

Les wasn't sure that he could hug him, but when the younger man pulled him into his arms, it was all Les could do to remain standing. Love, he knew, knew no bounds, and this was what he needed more than he did the next beat of his heart, or to fill his lungs with much needed air.

"Da, have you been here long?" He said that he'd been here an hour. They were letting them stay as long as they wanted now. "She's not going to make it, is she? Baby Bryn is going to die."

"Yes." That single word, even though he knew that she was going to die, cost him everything in his body. Falling to the floor, Les let all his sorrow out as he told his son what he'd told Bryn only moments ago. That he was going to make it up to all of them.

Going back to the room with Bryn, Walker sat on one side of her, Les the other. He told his son that he'd contacted the other two, and Walker said that he'd spoken to both of them.

"Addie wouldn't have been able to come if you'd not sent her the money. I only could just afford it. I have a wife now, and a baby on the way." A grandchild — something that Bryn had always wanted. Not children, she'd told him when she was about ten, just grandchildren. "Kitty is driving. I would have thought that she would have beaten me here."

Almost as if he'd summoned her, Kitty was dressing in the room. While she was there, Addi joined her. His children where all here — all of them that he didn't deserve. Les went to the little room to hug them as well, but Kitty wouldn't allow him to touch her.

"I'm not here for you, but for Bryn. And when things are settled here, I'm going back home. I want no reunion with you, Da. You had your chance and tossed us aside. I'm only here for my sisters and brother." He nodded. "And while I thank you for the cash. I'm going to be sending it back. When I needed you all those years ago, you sent us away. You're no longer allowed to try and buy me off. Just don't."

Les knew that it was no less than he deserved. Addi held him, told him that she was glad that he'd helped her today. And when this was finished, she told him, she wanted to have dinner with him, if he didn't mind.

"Never. I would love for us all to be able to get together." Addi told him not to worry about Kitty, she'd talk to her. It only just then occurred to him that they'd all been talking to each other. For that, he was grateful. At least they had tried more than he had.

They talked among themselves for the next hour. He knew that, like him, they knew that Bryn wasn't going to walk away from this. However, they talked as if she was going to get up and talk to them any moment now. They talked to her as well. Not like he had, feeling sorry for himself and talking like he was to blame for everything that had happened to her.

They spoke of picnics now that the weather had turned. About the things they were going to do this summer. Walker talked about his baby coming soon, how his wife was as excited as him. Again, Les had not been a part of that life, seeing his son marry, but he didn't comment. This was about them and their sister.

Not that they didn't talk to him too. Addi showed him pictures of her work, the art that she was doing to keep herself in food. Walker showed him pictures of his wife and their little apartment. Les made a mental note to send them more money, and a large gift to the baby.

Kitty, however, didn't say anything to him about her personal life. Not that he didn't know about it. That was something else that Dane had provided for him—information on his children, things that he wouldn't have known otherwise. Kitty was days away from losing everything she owned. Not for lack of trying, but she was just too smart for any job that she worked on, and when she tried to make changes, they would fire her. And she was brilliant, too. Dane had also provided the grades they'd had in college.

Twice more Bryn's machines went off. Both times it was over before the staff was able to come in. But each time they made sure that she had plenty of morphine to keep her comfortable, and that the fluids were flowing. After the second time, a doctor asked to speak to them—he came into the room, not even bothering with a gown.

"Her breathing is done by a machine. The monitor over her head is measuring her brain waves. When she was admitted to this hospital, she had a great deal. Then as her body began to try and heal itself, other functions began to shut down." He asked him what he was trying to say, to just say it. "That the women you knew and loved is gone."

Addi and Kitty started crying, and he glanced at them to see that Walker was holding them. He too was crying.

Les looked back at the doctor. He was showing them the screen that measured such activity.

"What is it you're suggesting we do, Doctor?" He handed him a form that had been filled out already. It was a copy of a donor card that had been filled out by Bryn several months ago. It also had a paper that was signed by her that said she didn't want to remain on a ventilator, nor be hooked up to anything just to extend her life. "You want us to end this for her."

"Yes. I do. Not for me, but you should know that while she was burnt badly and her intestine was also damaged, there are parts of her that we can still use." Kitty told him to get out. "I'm sorry about this, miss, but this is a decision that your father must make. She said that if he were alive, he would be the one to, in her words, pull the plug."

"You have no right to do this. None at all. You shoved her away, all of us, and you will not make the decision to kill her or not. No, I won't allow you to end her life, not while there is still hope." Les told Kitty that there wasn't any hope, not any more. "Shut the fuck up. You don't get any rights that has anything to do with us. She's been there for all of us, and you've been sitting in your mansion, just —"

"That's enough." He had never raised his voice to his children. Never had he spanked them. But right now, that's just what he wanted to do to Kitty. "You think this has been easy on me? To stay out your lives? If you think for one moment that I actually did that, you're harder than I thought you were. Meaner too. Who do you think got you into college on that scholarship? You had the grades, but you didn't have the money to get your books, did you? Then all of a sudden, you were okayed for that as well."

He looked at Addi. "Helping you was more difficult, but I did what I could. You moved around so much, just picking up and leaving, I had no idea where you were most of the time. But when I did find you, I made sure you had funds. The grocery store that you were in, you won that gift card that I know fed you for several months. Then you were gone again. I was always there for all of you."

"You paid for our car to be replaced, didn't you?" Les

nodded at Walker's question. "It had been totaled. Not our fault, but my wife, Cindy, had just found out that she was going to have a baby. And if I didn't work, have a car to get there, I'd lose my job."

"I didn't know you were married. I only helped when I could. You getting married wasn't told to me, but you can bet that I'm going to find out why." Les turned to Kitty. "Honey, I knew about the baby."

"No." He nodded. "No one was there for me. No, that's not right. I didn't want anyone around me. No one knew. I didn't want anyone to know that I'd been a failure at even that."

"What makes you think you're a failure? You're not, as far as I can see. None of you are. Despite having me as your father, you still made it through college. You worked hard, and you certainly made something more of your life than you should have. I would have given you everything had I been able. Anything."

The doctor cleared his throat and asked him what he wanted to do. "I'd like a few minutes with my family, if you don't mind. It won't be long, I promise."

The doctor left them, telling them that he would be at the nurses' desk. But a decision had to be made soon if they were going to have anything viable that they could use to help others. And that, more than anything, was what Bryn wanted for this part of her life.

Walker spoke first. "Bryn didn't want this. We all know that. She's fought the fight, and now it's done. I think, and this could just be me, but I think that she's only waited this long, held on for this time, because she wanted us all to come see each other." Kitty asked him why he'd think that. "Because when I got here, she coded once. Then twice more when you two arrived. It was as if she was saying to me, 'okay, I've got you here, now fucking do something about it.'"

Kitty laughed, and Les smiled as he spoke again. "I need to end her suffering, but I won't if you don't want me to. I think that this has to be an agreement between us all. As the doctor said, she's not here any longer, but just a shell that we're holding to us. I'm sick of being selfish when it comes to the wants and needs of you children."

When they all agreed, the doctor and two nurses came in to assist. They weren't asked to leave, as he thought they would be. But each of them held her—a hand, a touch to her leg, anything they could hold onto for one more moment. Les nodded when they said they were ready.

~*~

Wyatt walked through his home. He knew that it was inevitable that he was next to find a mate—not that he minded all that much. There wasn't any way that he could even hide away from someone coming to claim him. Wyatt had no delusions that he would do the claiming. He wanted it that way.

The house was paid off. He was also in the process of purchasing the land around him. He also owned another house on the land, but he didn't know what to do with it yet. It was within walking distance of this house.

He'd been thinking of just having it torn down. Not that it needed all that much work, but the taxes were higher because of the fact that it was improved land. But the little house might come in handy. What if his mate, he thought, kicked him to the curb? He'd like to know that he would have a roof over his head.

His phone was ringing when he got to the upper level. He rarely slept up there. The master suite was in this part of the house, as was a nursery. Neither part had appealed to him to sleep in. The second level was several bedrooms—five, as a matter of fact. Three bathrooms, as well as a large open space that had beautiful windows that showed off the spectacular back yard and the wooded area beyond. That was where he was standing when the service bell rang for him. Going to the intercom, he asked Blake what he needed.

"Mrs. Daniels called. She said that she's in labor again. I assured her that she had plenty of time, as she's only four months pregnant. New mothers—they're funny, aren't they, sir?" He laughed with Blake, a man that he had become friends with while he'd been in the service. "I have told her to go on to the hospital if she feels any worse in an hour, and that they'd call you with any tests they run."

No one knew his house number. Upon leaving the kitchen after having himself a nice dinner, he'd left his cell phone down with Blake. The calls to it had been transferred to the phone in his bedroom that he'd been using. But he hadn't felt like answering just yet.

"Tell her that I'll be in if they feel she needs me. And believe it or not, Blake, this is her fourth child. She was like this with the other three too."

Wyatt sat down on the chair that had been left behind when he'd moved in. The view was just too beautiful to ignore.

Wyatt must have dozed off. He knew that what he was seeing was only a dream. The woman in the dream with him had a blurred face, and she was a redhead. Wyatt had a real love of redheaded woman, and the temper that came with them.

196

"You have done it again, haven't you?" He smiled at the woman, seeing himself there like he was an intruder. "Why are you buying seeds that it's too early to plant? I told you, we have to wait for several more months, Kyle."

That wasn't his name, not even close. It took him a moment to realize that it wasn't him that the woman was talking to, even though he was there, but a little boy. He moved around the room, the kitchen that was nothing like the one he owned, and sat down. Once he was sure that the man winked at him, but he was sure that was just part of the dream. And that he wasn't really there any more than Wyatt was.

"But we can start them in the house, can't we?" The woman turned to take something out of the oven, and he had the most wonderful smell of chocolate chip cookies come to him. "Momma, when do you think that I'll be big enough to drive? I'd be able to run to the store for you."

"You still have some growing up to do. Now, I want you to get cleaned up and help me for a moment. Dr. Stanton will be here to check on your sister soon, and he will take some cookies in trade. I don't know what we'd do without him about." He wondered about the sister and how she was when she came into the room. "Oh, Milly, you do be careful around the stove, all right?"

"Yes, Momma." He watched Kyle help his sister to the table, and he snitched her a cookie off the cookie sheet. "Thanks, Kyle. Can you get me some milk too? But only a little bit. Mom needs it to make dinner, okay?"

Kyle pulled a box of powdered milk out of the cabinet and the jug from the refrigerator. When he had enough water in it, he measured out the powder to make the concoction. But Wyatt knew, as surely as he was watching them, that the ratio was wrong. That, too, was being cut back on for lack of money.

Wyatt had no idea why he was dreaming of this—not the children or the woman. He didn't know anyone with two kids with that name. Nor did he know all that many redheads.

When there was a knock at the door, Wyatt woke up from his dream and looked around.

"Wyatt, are you all right?" He told his dad, who was sitting across from him on the floor, that he was fine. Then asked him why. "You were talking. About a redheaded woman. And cookies. I brought you some, by the way. Mom was baking, and I thought of you. Are you all right?"

"Yes." He took two of the cookies from the tin and told him what he'd been dreaming about. Then Wyatt told him about him winking at him in the dream. "It was weird, Dad, like he knew that I was invading this time, and he wanted to make sure that I knew it."

"Maybe he did." Wyatt just frowned at his dad. "No, listen to me a minute. There are times, I tell you, that as a doctor I get those kinds of things. You know, a twinge of something here or there. Once when I'd been at a lady's house, she asked me to get her kitty. When I went out looking for the thing, I didn't find it. but I did find a little boy that had been hurt by falling out of the tree. After I got him all fixed up and on the way to the hospital, I went back to tell her that I'd not found the cat and I had to go. She said that she'd not sent me out to find her cat. In fact, she didn't even have one. So, I'm thinking that as a physician, you're just more prone to finding little things like that. The dream? Well, I'm not sure what to tell you about it. But I'd keep it in my memories. Just in case you might need it."

After talking to Dad about the reasons he'd stopped by, Wyatt headed out to the back deck of his home and stripped down to his bare skin. The pool was heated year-round, but it had been turned off for a couple of weeks now. Diving into the water, he nearly screamed, the water was so cold. But after getting used to it, he swam like he had in college — like he was in one of the races and he needed to win.

After doing ten laps, he got out and shifted. Running as his cat, he was forever aware of others that might be around. Keeping his nose to the air, he could smell all the changes in the earth. The freshness of the grass. The flowers that were making their way to the surface.

There was a pond back here that he would stock every summer, and couldn't wait to make time with his brothers to come here and spend the day. He'd even put electric back here to a small hut. That way they could have food and drinks. It also held the chairs that they used, as well as any fishing equipment — if they got around to fishing.

Checking out the hut to make sure that it was still locked up, he run for another hour before heading to the house. Getting into the pool again was tempting, but Wyatt was sure that he stank, so he bypassed it to go into the basement and shower there.

Putting the towel around his waist, he walked up to his room and laid on the bed. He usually slept in the buff, and when he opened up his window, he thought tonight was a good night for that. Rolling to his back, he closed his eyes. Wyatt was asleep before the first breeze blew across his body.

Before You Go...

HELP AN AUTHOR

write a review

THANK YOU!

Share your voice and help guide other readers to these wonderful books. Even if it's only a line or two your reviews help readers discover the author's books so they can continue creating stories that you'll love. Login to your favorite retailer and leave a review. Thank you.

AWARD WINNING, BESTSELLING AUTHOR

Kathi Barton, winner of the Pinnacle Book Achievement award as well as a best-selling author on Amazon and All Romance books, lives in Nashport, Ohio with her husband Paul. When not creating new worlds and romance, Kathi and her husband enjoy camping and going to auctions. She can also be seen at county fairs with her husband who is an artist and potter.

Her muse, a cross between Jimmy Stewart and Hugh Jackman, brings her stories to life for her readers in a way that has them coming back time and again for more. Her favorite genre is paranormal romance with a great deal of spice. You can visit Kathi online and drop her an email if you'd like. She loves hearing from her fans. aaronskiss@gmail.com.

Follow Kathi on her blog: http://kathisbartonauthor.blogspot.com/

Made in the USA
Coppell, TX
18 January 2020